Also by Amy Lukavics:

Daughters unto Devils

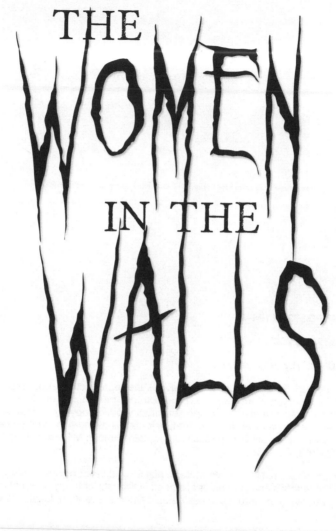

THE WOMEN IN THE WALLS

AUTHOR OF *DAUGHTERS UNTO DEVILS*

AMY LUKAVICS

HARLEQUIN®TEEN

ISBN-13: 978-0-373-21194-4

The Women in the Walls

Printed in U.S.A.

For Roxie, who has peered beyond the walls
of my very weird brain and still loves me anyway,
and for Joanna, who is always quick to point out my strengths
when I've forgotten what they are.

ONE

WALTER THE COOK killed himself in his little bedroom downstairs, just a few hours after saying good-night.

"Have sweet dreams tonight, little Lucy," he said to me that night, just as I was heading up the stairs after dinner. He'd called me "little Lucy" ever since his first day at the estate, and never really stopped after that. "I'll make you and Miss Margaret some eggs Benedict in the morning."

The more I think about it, the less sense it makes. What possibly could have happened in that time?

I'm the one who found him, but I can't really talk about it with my father, or my cousin Margaret, or my aunt Penelope. Nobody wants to know about the color of Walter's face after he'd been hanging from the beam for hours, the buckle of his black leather belt hardly visible through the swollen puffs of flesh that billowed around it. Or about how his hands looked like latex gloves filled with a lumpy sort of liquid. Or about how awful the room smelled from the mess he'd left in a splattered puddle directly beneath his shoes, his toes pointed to the floor like a dancer's.

Walter made every birthday cake I've had since I was four years old, every holiday dinner, every sick-day soup. Without any family of his own, he'd simply become a part of ours. Even Margaret loved him, which says a lot.

Margaret doesn't really like anybody.

Regardless, nobody wants to linger on the details when it's easier to move forward as if they're rumors instead of memories. That's how it's always been here, I guess. So ever since I found Walter dead, I've been acting as if nothing happened, even though on the inside I'm beginning to unravel, slowly, like a thread being pulled painstakingly from its spool.

Something isn't right in this house.

From the road, there is a narrow dirt path that snakes through trees and shrubs until it ends at a black iron gate with spiked posts that reach nearly twenty feet high. From there, a wide cobblestone path leads itself down the side of the manicured courtyard, then to the house that stands behind it at three full stories tall. There are fourteen bedrooms total.

The harsh appearance of the stone walls is softened

by sweeping curtains of ivy that are draped over the sides of the house like a cape. The roof is laid with beautiful red tile, and the accents around the windows and doors are made from black iron, like the fence. Beyond the open land that's sprawled behind the courtyard, there is a pine forest that stretches out and up into the rocky gray cliffs of the mountains.

It's a historical landmark, an estate of dreams that's been in my family for generations.

A few days after Walter's death, my aunt Penelope calls me into her bedroom while Margaret is taking a bath upstairs. Once I'm inside, she asks me to close the door. The inside of the room is a weird balance of messy and neat; the flowered bedspread is pulled smoothly over the mattress, but there are random stacks of dust-covered books all over the plush carpet, likely from the library on the second floor. Penelope is always reading one thing or the other.

"How are you doing?" she says, patting the bed next to her. Her face is relaxed, as if she's just had a few glasses of wine. I sit, slowly breathing in the scent of her lemongrass hand lotion. I love Penelope as much as I would have my own mother, if she hadn't died when I was three. The black hole of grief that should have bloomed inside me never had much time to develop or take hold, since my aunt moved herself and Margaret in within a few months to help my father take care of me. She filled the maternal role effortlessly, instantly.

I love her more than I love my father.

"Okay," I say, my smile forced. Penelope frowns at the sight of it.

"I know it couldn't have been easy on you, finding Walter like that." She lets out an irritated sigh. "It's not fair that it was you. I'll never forgive him for that."

I want to say that maybe it's we who need to be forgiven, not Walter, but I can't find a way how.

"I just don't understand *why*," I croak, my eyes growing hot. "Why would he do that in the first place? I thought he was happy here with us."

"People can be happy and sad at the same time," my aunt says. "Sometimes the sad parts just spiral out of control."

I wonder why she didn't talk to me about this sooner, like the day it happened, when I needed to hear it the most. Then I feel an instant, searing guilt for expecting her to coddle me so much; Aunt Penelope would never whine to someone else like this, bore them with her personal issues.

For an Acosta must never lack control. She must keep her back straight, and her clothes ironed, and her expression placid. She must refuse to be seen unless her hair and makeup have been set. She wears her armor like scales on a snake: patterned, impervious, perfect. She understands that smiling is tactical, that words are for getting things that you want, that tears have no use except to expose disgusting, snotty shortcomings.

"Well, it had to be someone that found him," I say, shifting my weight on the mattress. "I'll get over it."

"Sure, of course," she responds. Her dark braid hangs over her shoulder, nearly reaching her stomach. According to the photos I've seen, Penelope and my mother looked a whole lot alike. "I just want you to know I'm here for you, all right?"

Penelope reaches her arm around me, pulls me close. After a moment of resistance, I give in and lean my head against her shoulder. The scent of her sweater is sweet and clean from laundry softener.

"Everything's all right," she says softly. "Don't you worry about a thing."

I wish she was like this more often, like how she was when I was young. The past few years she's been colder and more distant, especially around me and Margaret. I'm starting to wonder if the stresses of the club are finally getting to her.

It's just a stupid country club, I think for probably the millionth time in my life. *How did it get to be as important to her as it is?* And it's not just Penelope who practically worships this lifestyle, but my father, as well. They're both always scrambling to keep up with the game of showcasing themselves at all the lavish dinners and cocktail hours, endless moments of opportunity to prove just how perfectly everything in their life is going.

It's all lies, of course.

The girl lives in a beautiful dollhouse made of stone, I wrote one time in my diary when I was young, my handwriting shaky but sure. *But underneath her shining plastic smile, there are only screams.*

"I've got to go," I say suddenly, standing and pulling myself away from my aunt's embrace. "I wanted to clean up my room before our tutor arrives."

"That's fine," Penelope answers. "I love you, Lucy." She hasn't said it in months.

"Love you," I say, the words soapy from disuse. I've always wondered what it would be like to use the phrase freely, without hesitation or embarrassment, especially because of how much I truly love my aunt.

Without another word, I go out through the front parlor and head up the wide staircase to the second floor, where my bedroom sits adjacent to Margaret's. The light coming from beneath the bathroom door tells me that my cousin is still bathing. Good. I need to be alone right now.

Once my bedroom door is locked behind me, I take a deep breath and head over to the decorated cigar box that sits in plain sight on the shelves surrounding my vanity. I take it down and bring it with me to my bed.

Whenever my brain goes bad from all the Acosta pressure, and the expectations gather and gather until they're ready to bubble over and stain everything with their mess, this box saves me. I made and started using it years ago, when I was maybe ten. Whenever anything bad happened after that, the box was able to fix it, make sure I remembered that I was still here, in this house, alive. In my head, I call it my magic box.

And, more recently, when Margaret asked me what was inside it, I showed her.

I showed her the inside of the box, which was filled with razors and lighters and pins. I showed her the frenzied tallies on my upper thighs that counted each and every word that I was never allowed to speak, every whimper that had to be muffled by the back of my arm, every question I wanted to ask but knew would only be met with silence and a change of subject.

And I showed her how I open my skin instead of my mouth, let the wounds weep blood while my eyes stay dry. *It's soothing*, I told Margaret. *It helps keep things dead inside when everything is too much to handle.* It isn't pretty or poetic, I made sure she knew. *It's just me doing my best.*

"But what if you cut too deep?" Margaret asked back then, eyeing the thicker, darker scars among the newer, redder ones. Their number was always rising, five, ten, fifteen, twenty. "What if you take it too far?"

I stared into her eyes as if the answer was obvious. "Well, then," I said without blinking. "If I take it too far, I guess that means I get to stop counting."

We never talked about it again.

By the time Margaret gets out of the bath and asks if I want to watch a movie in her bedroom, I've stopped caring all about finding Walter dead, and I've stopped caring about saying *I love you* to my aunt, and I've stopped caring about the little girl in the dollhouse made of stone whose head is forever swimming in her own silent screams.

Sometimes things just *are*, and all that's left to do is exist in spite of them.

"Sure," I call to my cousin through the still-locked door, returning the jeweled cigar box to its place on the shelf. The bandage across the back of my knee is hot and wet beneath my black leggings. "I'll be right there."

TWO

FIVE DAYS AFTER Walter died, my aunt Penelope walked into the forest behind the house and never returned.

I was in the library the afternoon she walked out, saw her go into the woods from the floor-to-ceiling windows of the second floor of the house. My aunt wasn't wearing a sweater despite how chilly it was outside, which I thought was strange but stupidly brushed off. I was doing an art project from my homeschool curriculum and told myself that I'd continue to work on it only for as long as Penelope was out for her walk. When she came back, I would finish my history essay before stopping for the day.

So I watched and watched for her as I waited for the glue to dry on the cuts of cardboard my fingers were pinching together, red glitter still gathered in clumps in the sides of my nails. I didn't think I'd get any further than the gluing, but before I knew it, the project was complete, and the moon was rising, and my aunt had never come back inside.

That's how I know she didn't return to the house unnoticed, only to catch a ride with some mysterious stranger who would take her someplace far away from here, leaving her keys and wallet and life behind. That's how I know that right now, at this very moment, my aunt is outside in the dark, surrounded by trees and pine needles and wolves. I don't know if she's hurt, or dying, or dead.

It has to be one or the other by this point. Days have passed.

It forces me to think about too many things. *Some of us die afraid,* my mind whispers, shaky at the knowledge, desperate for release from it. *Some of us die in awful, unexpected ways.*

The thoughts spiral in and out of each other, unlocking other thoughts, each more upsetting and heavy than the last. *First my mother, then Walter and now Penelope. I'm going to die one day. Everybody will.*

How is it going to happen? Will I be afraid, in pain, crying out for mercy? Will I be trapped in a small space, my mind racing helplessly as water rises around me, or will my head be crushed under the weight of stone from a collapsing building? Will I be raped and murdered? Will a bear strip the flesh from my bones and force me to listen as he eats me alive? Will it take an instant or a minute or an hour or...

"Stop," I whisper out loud from where I sit in front of the window in the cold shadows of the library, all the lights off, the sun finally setting. I've been sitting here since lunch, staring out at the woods, waiting, hoping, spiraling. "Please stop."

But it doesn't. It never does, and before long the thoughts drive me out of the dark silence of the room, to the other side of the second floor, where my bedroom sits one down from Margaret's.

"Marg?" I say, knocking on her closed wooden door with my knuckles. I try desperately to sound calm, together, *sane*, shove the hysterical questions so far down inside myself that I no longer know where they are. "We should eat dinner in my room tonight. We can watch sitcoms to take our minds off everything. I don't know about you, but I'm pretty desperate for some—"

"I don't want to," comes Margaret's reply from the other side. "I want to be alone."

It's the same thing she said last night. The first few days after Penelope disappeared, we didn't leave each other's sides. We didn't cling to one another and cry like we used to when we were much younger and too little to understand why it was important to control our weaknesses, but we stayed together, hour after hour, as if to prove to each other that neither of us was alone in the chaos of Walter's death and Penelope's disappearance.

But now she's pulling back, away from me. Why? I need her. We need each other.

"Are you sure?" I try again, clenching my teeth together as I anticipate what I know is coming.

"I'm sure," Margaret says. "I'm just going to go to sleep early again."

Then, silence. I bite at my lip impulsively as I make my way down the hallway, to the stairs that lead to my father's study. *Will I die from a sudden illness, like cancer?* I think wildly, my breath quickening uncomfortably. *Will I accidentally fall down the stairs and break my neck?*

"Dad," I say from the doorway of his study once I've reached it, a little more urgently than I intend. He's sitting with his head bowed over a big paper spread out over the desk and simply grunts in answer.

I take a step closer and see that the paper is a map of the grounds and surrounding area. Over the forest, there are six white pins spread over the end closest to the house.

"What's this?" I say, turning my neck to get a closer look.

My father lights his pipe and stretches his back, his eyes never leaving the paper. "This is all the ground we've covered looking for Penelope," he mumbles, smoke sneaking out between his lips as his fingers move over one pin to the other. "How can I help you?"

"I was just wondering if you were going out to look for her again tomorrow," I say, a lump rising in my throat. I push it down without showing any evidence of its presence. "I wanted to make sure everything is being done. Why haven't the police brought dogs or something? Why are you and your friends putting more effort in than they are? Don't they understand that she's *out there?*"

Come to think of it, I realize, *I haven't seen a single officer yet.*

"We're doing what we can," my father promises, avoiding eye contact as he usually does with me. It's like looking at me for too long hurts him in some way. "And we don't have any plans to stop the search until we find an answer. As hard as it is, we need to be patient, Lucy."

"Right," I say, hearing the truth but not wanting to accept it. It's all becoming so unbearable, especially with Margaret starting to pull away. "I'm glad that you're still at it. That's all I wanted to know."

Last night I had dreams that Walter was following me around the house, dead, looking just as he did when I found him hanging from the ceiling. He wasn't saying anything in the dream, just staring at me with a confused expression as I tried to go about my schoolwork and chores as if he wasn't there. But after a while he started tapping on my shoulder with one lumpy, swollen finger, urgently, demanding for me to look up.

When I did, he stared into my eyes without blinking, tilting his head to the side. *Where is Penelope?* he mouthed, soundless, his throat too ruined to speak. When I told him that she was gone, his expression turned from confusion to rage. Just as he looked like he was going to lean forward and tear my face apart with his bare hands, I woke with a start.

"We are definitely still at it," my father confirms, bringing me back to the map and the pins and the heavy smell of pipe tobacco. "Go on with the rest of your night now. You and Margaret get some rest."

For all my life, it's always been *you and Margaret get some rest*, or *you and Margaret entertain yourselves for now, can't you see I'm busy?* or *you and Margaret are making too much noise upstairs.* But now it's just me. I tell myself that I'll have an answer soon, that someone will find something in the next few days for sure, and one way or the other, we can bring some degree of closure to this situation.

As I'm walking to my own bedroom, I hear a strange sound coming from Margaret's: laughing. Instead of opening my door, I go to hers and listen. She's giggling all right, high-pitched and shrill and ringing with joy. The laughs are muffled, as if she's covering her mouth with her hands or a pillow to hide the sound. "I could kill her," I think I hear her say.

"Margaret?" I say, knocking sharply. The laughter stops abruptly. "What are you doing?"

Silence for a few moments. I look down to the bottom of the door—her light is still on. For a minute

I think she isn't going to answer, but then I hear her footsteps coming across the room for the door. She opens it. Her black hair is mussed as if she came straight from bed. Her eyes are shiny and wide.

"What do you want?" she demands. "Why are you here again?"

I try not to show how much her questions sting.

"What were you laughing at just now?" I ask, desperately wishing she'd invite me in. "I thought you were going to bed."

"I *was* in bed, Lucy." My cousin sounds irritated. "And I wasn't laughing. I don't know what the hell you're talking about."

What? "I heard you," I say slowly, my eyebrows furrowing at her lie. "I know I did. And your light was on. You said, 'I could kill her.'"

"Look, I've been sleeping with the light on lately, all right?" She is frowning. "Stop looking for reasons to come bother me. You're being annoying."

In my head, I know that Penelope's disappearance should be something that brings Margaret and me closer together. We should still be sticking together, lying around in our rooms while we swap theories on what exactly happened to my aunt.

"Are you mad at me or something?" I blurt. "How come you want to be by yourself so much all of a sudden?"

Can't you see I'm barely holding on? I want to yell, but a true Acosta would never admit such a thing.

"Because I need some time to think," Margaret says. She crosses her arms over her stomach and narrows her eyes in just the slightest. "How is that not understandable to you?"

My cheeks flush in embarrassment. I suddenly see myself as she sees me: unable to handle my own shit. Pathetic. *Weak.*

"I'm sorry," I mumble. "I'll just...see you around."

She closes the door in my face. I walk to my bedroom, forcing myself to take slow, easy steps. *I'm fine,* I think as my eyes begin to burn and sting. I close the door behind me and look over my room, perfectly neat, everything in its place. The sight of it brings just a touch of relief. Then I see the bejeweled box on the vanity shelf, the magic box of razor blades. *Not today,* I think with a sniff, defiantly turning my head away from it. *I can handle myself today just fine, thank you.*

I put on my pajamas and turn off the light and crawl beneath the thick down comforter on my bed, the satin sheets heaven on my exposed skin. I spend a good while trying to mute out the sound of my own brain, begging it not to send me another dream with Walter in it, pleading for it to think about anything but Penelope or Margaret for just one moment...

But it doesn't. Instead, it washes over me with questions, and thoughts and violent visions that will never come to be but feel like they're happening, anyway. I think about Margaret laughing giddily in her room alone. I think about Penelope walking into the woods with her back turned to me. I think about Walter; I think about dying.

But more than anything, I think about the ever-growing suspicion that something is very wrong in this house.

THREE

I THOUGHT I HEARD voices in the walls last night, but it was only the sound of Margaret crying from the next room over. I haven't heard her cry since we were ten. I wonder if she knew I could hear her. I wonder if she cared.

She hasn't talked to me at all about how badly she misses her mother. I don't exactly expect her to—we've never been the type to get *too* deep into feelings, being Acostas and everything, but I thought a situation this big might demand a little change on that front. When Penelope first disappeared, Margaret was all about staying close. But as the days passed, so did her moods. I can't help but feel like there's something she's hiding from me. Is it grief or something else? I think about the weird bursts of laughter coming from her room last night, followed an hour or so later by the crying. I wonder how much longer she'll act this way; how much longer I'll have to face my own mind alone in the quiet of this enormous house. I hope not for much longer.

When morning comes, Margaret doesn't show up to breakfast. If my father notices, he doesn't mention it, instead keeping his eyes on the newspaper spread out over the oak table, a scone and steaming cup of coffee nearby. I regard his pressed suit and gelled hairstyle with a frown. How did he conjure the will to give a shit about *cuff links* when he got dressed this morning, with everything that's been going on?

"Are you going to look for Aunt Penelope some more today?"

My father clears his throat but does not look up. "No, Lucy. We're finished. We've combed through those woods over and over again."

"But that can't be it," I say, starting to get worked up already. My defenses are starting to break down more easily with all this worrying about Margaret. "Nobody found her. She has to be out there somewhere. I saw her walking into those woods. She didn't even bring a coat with her. It was like she was taking a walk. This wasn't planned, Dad. She didn't run away, she's *out there* somewhere—"

"I'm tired of having this conversation," my father snaps, finally raising his eyes from the newspaper to bore them into mine. "If you need me to explain to

Margaret why the search party has officially ended, I would be happy to do so. That isn't your burden to bear."

I think of what he said to me before when I asked him about searching for Penelope. *We're doing what we can. We don't have any plans of stopping the search until we find an answer.* That promise sure lasted a hot minute. Why am I even surprised?

"I just think that we shouldn't give up so easily," I say in a low voice. "It's only been two weeks since she's been gone..."

"Lucy." My father sighs and takes a calculated gulp from his coffee mug. "Two weeks is a long time to be outside at this time of year."

Deep down, I know he's right. Scarborough Falls starts getting chilly in the beginning of October, and by November it's cold by day and frigid by night. We're almost at the end of November now. And with all the icy rain and sleet we've been having...

"Why don't you go check on your cousin?" my father says, interrupting my train of thought. "I don't think she's doing too well today. I found her mumbling to herself in the library this morning."

So Margaret *is* awake; she just chose not to come to breakfast.

"What do you mean, mumbling?" I ask, my eyebrow raised. "What was she saying?"

"I'm not sure," he says and takes a moment to sip his coffee. "I couldn't hear her very well."

The idea of Margaret mumbling to herself shreds my nerves to bits. "I'm sure she's just missing her mom."

I shift in my seat as I remember the fact that I haven't seen a single cop since we first noticed my aunt was missing. I assume the police must have come at least once to take a report, but I never saw them myself, although I suppose the house is large enough that they could have easily gone unnoticed by Margaret and me.

I know they never joined in on the search party in the forest with my father and about ten of the men from the country club, because I would have seen their squad cars parked on the cobblestone that surrounds the fountain out front, amid all the Jags and Bentleys and occasional vintage Cadillac.

It embarrasses me that I didn't join in on the search party. I was too afraid of finding Penelope dead, with her head cracked open on a rock, or throat torn out by an animal, or whatever it was that had prevented her from returning home to Margaret and my father and me. I kept seeing Walter's face in my mind, his gross hands, his smell; kept picturing my aunt in his place. Unbearable.

So instead of taking part in the search party, I stood at the windows of the library on the second floor, watching the line of richly dressed men descend into the shadows of the forest beyond the courtyard. As the days passed, fewer and fewer men showed up to go out with my father. The day before yesterday was the first day that nobody showed up.

I struggle to digest what my father said, about how they weren't going to look for her at all today. It's over, officially.

"Well, I guess I'll go look for Margaret," I say, breaking the uncomfortable pause. "It's good to know you've thrown in the towel so quickly. I wonder how Penelope would feel if she knew—"

"Lucy." My father's voice has a dangerous edge to it from behind the newspaper. The cuff links on his wrists have started trembling. "That will be more than enough."

I let the sharp metal edges of the chair legs scrape across the white marble tiles as I stand. My father doesn't react, and I storm out, almost jumping out of my skin when I round the corner and nearly walk straight into Margaret.

"Shit!" I exclaim under my breath. I raise my hand to my chest and instinctively lower my voice to a whisper so my father can't hear. "Were you listening in on that or something? What's been up with you?"

I notice that she's still wearing the same clothes she wore last night, her black curls hanging in stringy clumps that fall just past her chin. She licks her chapped lips and crosses her arms over her stomach.

"I have something to show you," she whispers back,

ignoring my questions. Her bare foot taps against the hard flooring of the front entryway. "Will you come with me or what?"

I want to wrap her up into a hug, tell her to take a shower and a nap and to eat a hot meal. I think of last night, of how stubbornly she pushed me away. If I say something to try to help her now, she'd just throw it back in my face. No, thanks. At least she's talking to me, asking me to follow her somewhere. It's already an improvement from yesterday.

We head to the triple-wide staircase in the back of the parlor, her just ahead of me, both of us silent. Since we were children, we'd creep through the house this way, exploring every room of every floor like mice. Now that we're seventeen, our home studies usually take up most of the day, but shortly after Penelope disappeared, we were granted permission to take an extended winter break.

I follow my cousin up the stairs to the third and highest floor. She leads me through one of the plushly carpeted hallways to the back corner of the house, where a miniature wooden staircase ascends steeply into an opening in the ceiling.

"The attic?" I say, uncertain. "What were you doing in the attic?"

I have a sudden flash of fear that she's about to let me in, *really* let me in, in a way that I might not be able to handle. *Tough shit,* I tell myself. *This is what you wanted—not to be alone in this.*

"Wait until you see this," she breathes, her eyes wide with excitement. "You're going to piss your pants."

She climbs the tiny staircase quickly, her wrinkled cotton skirt floating behind her, and I follow. The curiosity is powerful enough to cause me to shiver.

"I don't remember the last time I was in here," I remark after we've reached the top, rubbing my arms in the chill. "There are probably rats, Marg."

The single-bulb light that hangs from the ceiling is already on and fills the stale-smelling room with a faint yellow glow. "Rats." Margaret snickers, rushing to crouch beside the wall. "Sure. Come closer, you're too far away."

I walk to my cousin, looking around the attic for anything that appears strange or out of the ordinary that would make me *piss my pants.* The room is open and large, with a thin film of dust that covers everything from the floor to the walls to the stacks of boxes against the back that carry the belongings of my dead mother.

From here, I can see her name scrawled hurriedly over the side of one of the boxes. *Eva,* it says, and I shiver at the sight of it. The attic and its memories of the dead have always creeped me out.

On the wall opposite the one Margaret is crouched by is a large circular window that is blocked off by an elaborately carved cover of wood, latched shut and blocking out any detection of sunlight. The swirling green-and-gold Victorian wallpaper that accents the rest of the house is missing up here, which gives the attic a stripped, empty feel.

"Do you know what's on the other side of this wall?" Margaret says, grinning up at me.

"Um," I mumble, not sure what she's getting at. "The stone from the exterior walls?"

"Wrong," she whispers and knocks on the wood with three sharp taps. "Get a load of this."

"Margaret—" I start, but she shushes me.

My cousin waits with an odd intensity, her arm frozen in place with her fist raised just over the wall, as if she'll knock again. She doesn't blink. She doesn't breathe.

"Did you hear something before?" I offer gently. I feel awfully worried looking at her, all smudged and disheveled with dark rings under her eyes.

"This is bullshit," she whispers under her breath, her eyes growing wet. "She was here... It happened... She was here last night and this morning..."

"Who was?" I ask, confused.

"I have an idea," Margaret says, standing from her crouch. "I bet she isn't doing it because you're watching. Turn around and cover your eyes."

"What?" I take a step back, raising an eyebrow. "That's a little weird."

"Just do it," she urges, motioning me to turn with her hands. "If you peek, I'll fucking kill you."

My heart skips a beat at her words. She's never really talked to me like that before. I remember again what I thought I heard her say in her room last night: *I could kill her.*

"Fine," I say, uncomfortable but willing to go through with this, just to see what the hell Margaret is talking about. I turn slowly until I'm facing the covered window, take a deep breath and cover my eyes with my hands.

"Don't peek," she insists again.

"Jesus, Margaret," I snap, tired of her pushiness. "I said I won't, okay?"

I hear her knock on the wall again, somewhere behind me. Almost immediately, there comes a tiny swarm of little tapping sounds, moving all around the wooden surface. I frown beneath my hands, confused.

"Okay," I say slowly. "So I'm supposed to believe that wasn't y—"

The tiny tapping sounds suddenly turn into violent scratching noises, loud and hard enough that I fear Margaret's nails will rip and snap away from her fingertips. Startled, I lower my hands and begin to turn back around. *If you peek, I'll fucking kill you.*

"Don't turn around!" Margaret bellows, but I'm already facing her again. She stands near the wall, out of breath, and the sound has stopped abruptly.

"Are you okay?" I ask, stepping forward to inspect her fingers, but she pulls away from me.

"Don't you get it?" she says, her eyes wide. "That wasn't me!"

"Then why are you out of breath?" I ask, my voice quiet. She doesn't answer, instead looking down to the floor. "Why did you really bring me up here?"

"Oh, shut up and go away," she snaps, waving her hand at me without glancing up. "You couldn't make it any more obvious that you think I'm cracking up if you tried."

"No, I don't think that," I say quickly, too quickly. "I'm sorry, Marg, this is just kind of—"

Margaret lets out a joyless chuckle and waves me off. "Seriously, Lucy, go. I wouldn't want to waste your time with any of this. You know, maybe if you go stare out the library window some more, you can bring my mother back from the dead."

Her words cut me to the bone, causing me to flinch. I try to tell myself that she's just lashing out, that something is eating away at her, that she's just lost enough in her grief to become weirdly fixated to the most isolated place in the house.

"That's not fair," I start, and she tries to cut me off with another wave. I don't let her. "You can't blame me for hoping, and it's not like you're there for me." I blush when I realize that I've made it sound like she's the one who should be there for me, and not the other way around, if at all.

"I'm sorry," I say, trying to find the words to explain. "I just miss her. And I miss you, too."

What was she trying to prove with this whole thing? And how did she make those violent scratching sounds without tearing her hands up?

She stares up at me from where she sits crouched against the wall. "Lucy," she says, her voice flat. "I think it might be a little too late for you to tell me that."

"Margaret?" I respond, holding my hand out to her a little bit. *This is me trying*, I want to scream. "Please come out of this attic with me."

"Get out," comes my cousin's reply, and she leans forward to hold her ear against the wall. "Leave me alone."

Frustration seeps through my body as I realize that she's not going to budge. I thought that maybe she was starting to come out of her strangeness from the past few days, but clearly I was wrong. I don't know what to say to Margaret anymore, so I leave her without another word in the dusty, stale-aired attic, my mind still stumbling over the memory of the frantic clawing noises my cousin somehow made on the wall.

From the third-floor hallway, I make my way back to the main staircase, then get off at the branch to the second floor. Walking with purpose, I pass my own bedroom, then Margaret's, then an empty one that's used as yet another spare. I pull a hard right at the end of the hall and go into the library, toward the upholstered armchair I have dragged across the carpet to face the floor-to-ceiling windows that overlook the courtyard and forest beyond.

I sit daintily on the chair, my hands in my lap, my feet flat on the floor, my heart fluttering in my chest like a frenzied bird. I stare out at the forest, enveloped in silence, hoping with every breath that Penelope will step out from behind one of the trees and wave up at me, a smile on her face, yelling so loudly that I can somehow hear her through the glass: *the nightmare is finally over. Everything will be okay.*

But it's not, and it won't be, not ever again. *She's dead*, my mind screams at itself, louder and louder with each passing moment, the library agonizing in its silence. *She's dead and now everything has been completely ruined.*

FOUR

MARGARET ONCE TOLD me that our mothers hated each other.

She said that when our grandfather died, he left the entire estate to my mother, Eva, instead of dividing it up equally between her and Penelope. My aunt had been furious and would pick fights about it whenever she came over to let baby Margaret and me waddle together through the rows of rosebushes in the courtyard, the sun warm on our backs and chubby little legs.

Penelope wanted to move herself and Margaret out of their cramped apartment in town and into the enormous house along with the rest of us. There was more than enough space and several empty rooms, but still my mother repeatedly turned her sister down. She wanted the whole house to herself.

Something told me it wasn't as black-and-white as Margaret made it out to be, but I still feel an uncomfortable sort of shame when I think about it. This place was Penelope's childhood home. It couldn't have felt good to be turned away from it.

I leave the library after two agonizing hours, swearing to myself once again that I won't be returning anymore to just sit around and wait for nothing. I also can't be running to my room to find solace in my bejeweled cigar box as often as I have been lately. The number of scratches and scars on the tops of my legs and hips has risen too much. It's starting to feel like my skin can't breathe, like *I* can't breathe. I need to prove to myself that I am a true Acosta—show some control, get a grip.

I remember what I said to Margaret when we were younger and feel sick. *If I take it too far, I guess that means I get to stop counting.* I can't remember the last time I felt like I was the one choosing to use those razors. The previously comforting sheen of the box is almost antagonizing now. What have I done to myself?

I wander around the estate until lunchtime, where I eat in the grand dining hall alone. I dip my bread into my soup and look around the empty room of pillars and portraits nervously, stopping myself whenever I begin to wonder if Margaret has eaten yet.

No more, I think. *If she wants to stay away from me, I shouldn't push.* Clearly, she's chosen to go through all of this alone. Maybe I just need to accept that and give her the space right back.

There is a dark place inside me that wonders if Margaret is shutting me out because of how things were between her and her mother. Penelope and I were always closer, sharing more of the same interests and acting with similar attitudes that were so different than Margaret's, who didn't care as much about things like order or rules or tradition. Penelope rarely grew angry with me, or my father, but she was more often than not snipping back and forth with Margaret over this or that.

My father and Penelope never kissed or hugged or touched in front of Margaret and me, but between the curl of his half smile and the twinkle in my aunt's eye whenever we caught them chatting over lunch or tea in the courtyard, it was clear that neither of them was feeling too lonely.

The chemistry was practically electric, although Margaret and I almost never spoke of it to each other anymore, as I think we were both afraid of getting into an argument over it. Every time it would end with Margaret saying the same thing: *cousins are not supposed to be sisters.*

I spend the afternoon reading in my bedroom, where I accidentally fall asleep until it's dark. When I wake up, I expect to feel refreshed, but I'm somehow more tired than I was before I lay down. I go back downstairs to the dining room, where dinner has been served and my father and Margaret are eating in silence. It's a good thing I woke up on my own, because apparently neither of them were planning on coming to get me.

The candles in the middle of the table are lit, and a slow jazz record plays from out of the record player in the corner. Margaret's black hair is wet and combed back, and she's wearing a long-sleeved pajama set made of gold satin. Even though I'm still upset about what happened in the attic, I'm at least relieved to see her clean and comfortable.

Without meeting my cousin's eye, I sit in front of the empty plate at the end of the table and serve myself from the platter nearest to me, which is loaded with thick slices of roast beef and a small mountain of roasted potatoes and carrots. I take some salad and bread before pouring gravy from a tiny silver pitcher all over my meat and potatoes.

"Now that you're both here," my father says in between a bite of roast, "I can remind you that Miranda's daughter is going to be moving in tomorrow morning, in order to help with preparations for the upcoming annual holiday party for the club. She'll be staying in the spare room at the end of the hall on the second floor, the one just past Margaret's."

Neither my cousin nor I say anything. Miranda is the new cook who replaced Walter—her food pales in comparison, although I can't claim not to be biased.

Still, I couldn't care less about her daughter, just as long as she leaves me and Margaret alone. I hope she doesn't think that just because our rooms are close that we'll all be friends.

"There is also a smaller dinner party to be scheduled between now and then. Miranda won't be able to keep up in the kitchen with the demand for so much food, especially with Penelope gone. So that's where the cook's daughter comes in."

Of course! Walter is dead and aunt Penelope is missing, so obviously the task of utmost importance would be to make sure that the precious country club isn't inconvenienced at all. My dislike for all of those stupid old men just keeps on increasing. Can't they all just go out and get real jobs? How do they even make all that money to waste, anyway?

Margaret pours herself a glass of milk from the pitcher next to the bread but doesn't take a drink from it. I bet she's thinking the same thing that I am.

"There's also a more serious matter to discuss," my father says, clearing his throat. My heart skips a beat—has he learned something about my aunt?

"I need to know who ruined all of the photos in Penelope's room."

My mouth slacks open in shock, but Margaret keeps her eyes on her plate.

"What do you mean, *ruined*?" I ask. "What happened in Penelope's room?"

"Someone went into her desk and personal drawers and went wild with a permanent marker," my father says. "Priceless items have been ruined with scribbles and curse words."

I swallow my half-chewed bite of roast. *"What?"*

"I'm curious about something, Uncle Felix," Margaret says calmly, tearing soft white tufts of bread away from the crust and rolling them into balls between her fingers. "Why were *you* in her room, looking through her drawers?"

My stomach grows heavy with dread. If it really was Margaret who ruined Penelope's photos, she is starting to go off the deep end for sure.

My father's cheeks flush red. "Was it you who ruined her things, then, Margaret? Scribbled her face out in every picture she owned?"

Every picture she owned? I look at Margaret's stoic face, bewildered. What was she *thinking*?

"You didn't answer my question," she says, her voice steady. "So I don't see why I should have to answer yours."

"Did you do that?" I ask, unable to hold it in any longer. In addition to the worry I've felt over how she's been withdrawing and hanging out in the attic, now there's anger, too. Penelope doesn't belong just to Margaret. Those weren't her pictures to ruin, no matter how she was feeling.

"I never said I did it," she says to me, popping a piece of the bread in her mouth. "But thanks for assuming."

"Your mother loved you." My father stands from the table, apparently finished even though his dinner is only half-eaten. "I can't believe you'd do something so cold out of pure resentment. What are you mad at her for? You act like she left us on purpose!"

"You don't know the first thing about my mother," Margaret replies, her voice flat. "Neither of you do, and that's the problem."

"So you did it for attention?" I ask. "You're proving your point by ruining stuff that we can never get back?"

"You will not be allowed to act this way," my father cuts in. He's never had to take a parental tone with Margaret, and it shows in the clumsiness of how he talks. Despite his red face, he looks determined. "I would never dream of sending you to live elsewhere, but—"

"Of course you wouldn't," Margaret interjects. "But you still had to bring it up, right, Uncle Felix? To keep me in my place?"

Will every dinner be this way from now on? A sad little group of people at an enormous table who, it turns out, don't really know each other at all? It's not until now that I notice how heavily Penelope directed the tone during times like these. She was the one to calmly translate things between Margaret and my father, but

I don't know how to do that. I don't even *understand* Margaret right now, let alone feel equipped enough to step into this.

"You will stay out of her room," my father commands. "You will keep your hands off her things and you will respect me as your guardian."

"*Are* you my guardian?" Margaret asks, her tone almost challenging. "I feel like that's something that should have been worked out with the law by now. What did the police say, by the way? About my mother's disappearance? I certainly haven't talked to any officers, and you'd think that they'd want to question everyone to make sure nothing fishy was going on."

My father doesn't reply. I have to admit the question is legitimate, even if Margaret has been out of her mind between the attic and the photographs in Penelope's room.

"The police came and took the report the day after she disappeared," he insists after a moment, throwing his hands into the air. "What is it with you two and your suspicions? They didn't need to question either of you because there *wasn't* anything fishy about the situation. Clearly, she went for a walk and endured some sort of horrible accident. She may have been drunk, lost her way somehow..."

His voice wavers with emotion, causing his cheeks to instantly redden in embarrassment. I think about how he and Penelope used to look at each other, and feel a sick mix of sadness for my father and secondhand embarrassment from his quivering chin.

"Clearly," my cousin repeats, rolling her eyes. "Wow, you sure do seem to know everything, Uncle Felix."

"That's enough," he says, his face still red. "That's about as much as I can handle for one day. If there is just one thing I could ask of you girls for the next two weeks, it's that you'll stay out of my and Miranda's way while we learn how to continue with the party planning in Penelope's absence."

Then he's gone, his footsteps echoing and fading throughout the dining room and parlor as he makes his way to his study. Since my aunt disappeared, it's been startling, almost pitiful, how intensely my father is distracting himself with the country club. It's like the parties are suddenly the most important thing in the entire world, even more important than getting to the root of why Margaret ruined the photographs. I stare at my cousin through wide eyes.

"What the hell is going on with you?" I ask once she makes it clear that she intends to remain silent. "Why would you do that stuff to all of Penelope's photos? She's your mother..."

"You mean, she was," Margaret says. "She's gone now."

A lump forms in my throat. "I'm starting to worry about you," I say. "You never talk to me about anything anymore, you're acting different, and earlier in the attic—"

"Earlier in the attic I was trying to scare you," Margaret says dismissively. She stops chewing for a moment and reaches over for my father's glass of unfinished wine. I think back to when Margaret told me she had something to show me in the attic. She was so serious about the knocking on the wall, desperate even. I don't know if I believe that she was only trying to scare me.

After Margaret chugs the wine, she sets the glass down and goes back to her roast beef. "The truth is that I've been thinking a whole lot about my mom," she says. "And it's stuff I'm pretty sure you wouldn't want to hear. That's why I'm not talking to you."

"What do you mean, stuff I wouldn't want to hear?"

"Well," Margaret says. "You act as if she just vanished into thin air, instead of dying painfully, scared and alone."

Her comment is like a slap to the face, especially after all of the torture my mind has been putting itself through over this very topic. "How do you know she died painfully?" I ask, my voice nearly a whisper. *Why would she say that?*

Margaret does something startling then: she *smiles*, an unsettling and icy smirk that, for a brief moment, makes me feel as though I am looking into the face of madness. Suddenly my head feels light.

"Let's just say I have my ways," she says after the

pause. She wipes her mouth with a napkin and stands, smoothing the back of her satin pajama pants before facing me. "I'm going to bed now. Maybe we can… hang out tomorrow or something."

She hasn't suggested such a thing in days. I might be happy about the idea if it wasn't for the dreadful pit growing heavy in my stomach. Underneath the table, my feet are tucked nervously against one another. My chest tightens at the sight of her still-present smirk.

"Sure," I say quietly, desperate for the conversation to end. "Whatever you say, Margaret."

"Cool." She gives the top of my head a rough kiss before heading out toward the staircase. "Go to sleep, Lucy. And stop thinking about what happened to my mother. One way or another, death is painful for us all."

For five full minutes I sit alone at the table, too scared to move, too worried. The notion that Margaret had anything to do with my aunt's disappearance makes me physically ill. There is no way it could be real. At first I thought she was just acting strange because of grief, but certain things, like the attic and the ruined photographs and that icy smirk, make me feel like there's something that she's hiding. Something beyond the disappearance and bigger than her jealousy over how well Penelope and I got along.

I sift through memories in my head, looking for clues suggesting that my cousin is capable of anything sinister: Margaret glaring on as my aunt and I fawned over a gardening book together that my cousin had deemed dull, or Penelope praising me over my studies during dinner, while hardly acknowledging that Margaret had done just as well—if not better—with hers.

There were many instances like that, I know deep down. At the time I was always too happy to notice or care how Margaret felt—whenever I felt bad about it, the same bitter thought would come back to me, sour in my mind: *at least she's got a real mother.*

Still, the memories feel stranger now, darker. Is it because there's truth to my suspicions, or is it because I'm completely overcome with paranoia? *No, I decide, this is silly. I am just under a considerable amount of stress, and so is Margaret. There's an explanation for everything that's happened.*

Margaret could never kill anybody.

Maybe just one small cut, my mind whispers frantically as the panic fails to dissipate. *Go up to your room and let the pressure bleed out of you, just a little bit, just until your hands stop shaking…*

I nearly jump out of my skin when somebody enters the room from behind me. I turn with a gasp, only to see the cook standing beside a similarly featured girl who looks to be around my age. They are both wearing coats that are streaked with rain.

"I'm so sorry to startle you, honey," Miranda says.

"I was just bringing Vanessa through to her room. She arrived earlier than planned."

Despite my already-growing resentment for Vanessa, I'm at least grateful for the abrupt interruption of silence. It almost feels like someone caught me in the act of something unspeakable, even though there's no way for them to tell what was going through my head. The leftover shame simmers away slowly inside—*nothing happened, you did it, you stopped yourself.*

I know deep down that I just got lucky.

I take the girl in, the first peer besides Margaret whom I've seen in a few years, since we started doing our schooling at home. We hated school and the people in it, but not as much as they hated us. Whenever I started coming close to making a friend, Margaret would get jealous and ruin it somehow, earning herself a reputation for being weird and rude. I soon learned it was easier for everybody if I blocked people out from the start. Eventually we just stopped going altogether. It was better for us, Margaret insisted, and I agreed.

"Hi," the girl says and smiles at me. "You must be Lucy, or Margaret. Either way, I've heard all about you."

The girl is stupidly cheerful, causing me to feel validated in my preconceived notions about her. Does she not know the circumstances, the entire reason she's here in the first place? Why would she grin at me like she's on fucking vacation?

"It's raining outside?" I ask blankly, staring at the droplets of water falling from the ends of her dark blond hair.

"Yeah," Vanessa says, uncertainty evident in her voice as she takes in my bitter disposition. "It's been coming down pretty hard for the past hour. The drive was a nightmare."

I try not to imagine Penelope's body out there in the rain and take a minute to stare into the new girl's face, not caring too much that it might seem rude. "Oh," I say after a moment. She shifts her weight uncomfortably. "Well, I'm Lucy. Margaret's gone to bed already. I'm just about to turn in myself."

"You go on ahead, honey," Miranda says softly and steps up to pat Vanessa's hand. I think she can tell how on edge I am. "I can show Vanessa in just fine. You girls chitchat later."

Not on your life.

I nod and walk past them, grateful when I realize that Miranda is purposefully lingering behind so that they can walk separately. Knowing I have a minute before they follow, I quickly make my way up to the second floor, past my bedroom to Margaret's.

"Marg?" I say softly and knock on the door. No answer.

"I saw the new girl," I say through the door. "She came early, apparently. She's way too happy to be here and I'm pretty sure you won't like her." I pause, my insides turning when I remember the things my cousin said earlier. "Anyway, I guess I'll see you tomorrow."

Still no answer.

"Are you asleep already?" I open the door just a crack and peer in. The fireplace in her room is lit, but the bed is empty. I hear footsteps approaching and realize I don't have enough time to make it back to my room before running into Miranda and Vanessa again. Instead, I keep going down the hall, past the empty room where the hallway curves back to go past the library and around to the main staircase again. While waiting for the new girl to get into her room, I glance up the dark stairs to the third floor. *No way*, I think, shivering. *Margaret's just in the bathroom, most likely.*

But curiosity gets the best of me. I make my way to the top of the staircase, my blood already starting to run cold at the silence. My father's room as well as the cook's quarters are both down on the first floor. Nobody lives up here.

Still, there are tiny plug-in lights lining the halls, and by their glow I make my way to the back hallway. The carpet is freshly vacuumed as always, and the stillness and silence coming from the dark, empty spare rooms is looming. Vivid wallpaper surrounds me, its Victorian pattern strangely eerie in the shadows, *reaching*, as if I'm making my way through a tangle of invisible vines that are trying to keep me away from the back end of the house. With every step, it becomes harder to continue forward.

From somewhere in the dark ahead, I hear a sharp, short giggle—Margaret. I take a deep breath and turn the last corner, my heart leaping at the sight before me.

The small opening in the ceiling that leads to the attic is lit up, the glow from the single bulb inside shining down onto the miniature staircase positioned below.

After a moment of shocked silence, I hear footsteps circling the opening, slowly, cautiously, as if she knows that I'm standing down here in the dark.

She giggles again, and I turn on my heel and race back down to my room.

FIVE

WHEN I WAKE UP the next morning, I realize, before I've even had the chance to open my eyes, that I'm not alone in my bedroom. There is someone in here, *close*, breathing in long, jagged breaths, like they're struggling to stay calm. Startled, I open my eyes.

Margaret is standing at the head of my bed, her face shockingly blank, her eyes wide and her mouth slacked open as she leans over me. Her hair hangs down like a curtain, casting a shadow over one side of her face. I realize that I'm trapped between her and the wall that my bed rests against. The air is stale with my cousin's morning breath.

Enclosed in her fist is a pair of silver scissors, the elongated blades pointing at my throat.

"What are you doing?" I cry out, my voice still groggy from sleep. Eyeing the scissors, I lean back to sit up against the wall, away from the glistening silver shears. "Why do you have those?"

Margaret blinks then, like she's only just realized what she's doing. She looks to the scissors in her hand, a frown on her face, then turns to toss them onto my desk, like she can't stand to hold them for another second. They spin across the wood before coming to a hard stop against the side of some notebooks. When all is quiet, Margaret turns back toward me. She clears her throat.

"The new girl is here," she says. "I…wanted to tell you."

"I know," I say slowly, pulling the blankets up to my chest from where I lean against the wall. She hasn't stepped back from where she was standing—if I reached out, I could touch her. "I saw her last night. I tried to tell you, but you weren't in your room."

I don't think she was expecting that. She finally steps away from the bed, lingering in the center of the room. I breathe a long, slow sigh of relief as the panicked feeling of claustrophobia fades away. *What in the hell was that all about?*

"Am I supposed to care that you noticed?" she asks, her voice tired.

"I just thought you said you were going to sleep after dinner, is all."

"I was, okay?" She's getting mad, or possibly embarrassed. "I brought some bedding into the attic. I don't like sleeping in my room anymore."

I shiver at the memory of seeing the yellow light shining through the opening in the ceiling on the third floor. It's so dusty and stale in the attic, I can't imagine wanting to sleep in it. What's so bad about her bedroom? I suddenly become acutely aware of the scissors on my desk, the blades lit up as they reflect the morning sun streaming through the blinds. I don't like how her face looked just now, when she was holding them near my neck.

"Get up so we can go do stuff," Margaret says suddenly and makes her way to my vanity to inspect my various tubes of lipstick.

"What kind of stuff?" I ask. Then, because I can't let it go, "What were you doing before I woke up? With the scissors?"

Margaret leans up to the mirror, trying on a dark plum shade that complements her brown skin. "I was trimming my bangs in here while I waited for you to wake up. The scissors were on your vanity." From where she stands, she picks something up from the base of the mirror—a short clump of hair. "See?"

"But you weren't standing at the vanity," I say, confused.

"Yeah." Margaret drops the hair and continues with the lipstick. "I came over there because you started making noises."

"Noises?"

"Like you were having a bad dream," she continues.

"You started making really weird faces. I came to shake you awake, but you woke up on your own."

I think back to when I first woke up, before I opened my eyes. I could hear her breathing in the silence. My face was relaxed. Something's not right with the story, but the desperate way my cousin looks at me now is pleading *it's fine, it really is, please just let it go.*

"Look," Margaret says, her voice softer. "Did you want to hang out today or not? I don't want to be alone."

Neither do I, I realize. I think I've had just about enough of that.

"Okay." I give in, pushing the blanket away. Whatever had come over my cousin before has clearly passed by now, whether she was lying about what really happened or not. Clearly, something's on her mind, and she hasn't talked to me for this long in days. Maybe she's finally starting to let me back in.

Maybe she'll tell me what she's been hiding.

"Apparently, things around here are about to get crazy." Margaret lets out a soulless chuckle. "As if they haven't already. But seriously, how hard could it be to plan a stupid holiday party? They really had to bring another person in? Give me a break."

"So much goes into it," I say, defensive on behalf of my aunt. I scoot out of bed and stretch my neck to the side. "More than you'd imagine." Then, because her eyes have narrowed and I suddenly feel nervous at the idea of saying anything that could possibly remind her of Penelope, "It's completely ridiculous."

I think of how hard Penelope would always dive into the planning, drawing up centerpiece ideas and making lists and bookmarking recipes for hors d'oeuvres in her cookbooks. Of course Margaret wouldn't have paid attention to any of that, or cared. She thought the whole thing was stupid.

"Those old rich bastards from the country club are what's ridiculous," Margaret says. "I've never understood why Uncle Felix and my mother were so hell-bent on impressing them with all the parties and dinners. And their *wives*, oh my God, gag me now..."

She puckers her lips and pulls the skin of her temples straight up. "Have you seen my new face-lift, dear?" she says in a flawlessly shrill impression of a country club wife by the name of Nancy Shaw. "It's my tenth one! Whoever says you can't outrun age has clearly never met my wallet, am I right?"

I can't help but laugh at the display. "Pretty spot-on, I have to admit."

She takes a funny little bow, then straightens back up. "So are we going to do something or not?"

The ice might not be completely broken, but at least it's starting to crack.

"I'll need to shower and stuff," I say, cautiously optimistic about my cousin's possible turnaround. Maybe getting confronted about the photos last night helped her realize that she's taken things too far. Margaret flops down on my still unmade bed with a magazine and begins flipping through the pages. Seeing her stand over me with the scissors feels so far away now, like a weird dream.

"Whatever," she says. "Just hurry up."

I'm not so sure that it's safe to be truly relieved yet—she still slept in the attic last night. I get ready as quickly as I can, speeding through my shower so that Margaret doesn't have to wait on me any longer than necessary. I don't want anything to turn her mood back around.

"Done," I say after I've finished with my hair. I feel a strange sort of relief at the idea of being able to get back into our old routine, even if just somewhat. At this point, I'm desperate for things to feel even half-way normal. "Let's eat, I'm starving."

Margaret whines and throws the magazine down. "Let's just grab something quick and take a walk or something. Put a sweatshirt on."

"All right."

The dining room has already been cleared by the time we arrive, the table empty. We walk through to the short hall that leads to the kitchen, where Vanessa stands alone at the island peeling potatoes. She looks happy to see us, until Margaret walks right past her to the refrigerator without even a hello. My cousin opens the fridge and peers inside, grabbing two waffles from a foil-wrapped stack. Then she picks two links of sausage out of a sandwich bag and kicks the door shut.

"I'm Margaret," she finally says, then walks back over to give me my food. "This is Lucy."

"I know," Vanessa says as she peels. "Lucy and I met last night. Hi."

I give a weak smile.

"So what's the deal with your family?" Margaret asks, biting into her waffle. "How come your mom was so willing to drop everything and come live somewhere with people she'd never met before, just to cook for some country club parties?"

The girl slows down with the peeler, raising an eyebrow at Margaret. "Oh," she says, tilting her head to the side as if making her mind up about us. "She's in the middle of a gross divorce, so she was happy to leave it all behind."

It's hard to tell if she's more irritated or embarrassed.

"Bummer about that divorce," Margaret says with zero compassion. I knew she'd give the new girl a hard time. "So did she tell you that my mother went missing? She's dead. That's the real reason why *you're* here."

I'm chilled at the sureness in her voice when she mentions Penelope being dead. It reminds me of how she was talking about it all last night. The hope I felt earlier about Margaret's new mood grows weaker. Whatever it is that's bothering her, I'm at least glad she isn't taking it out on me for once, and also that Vanessa finally looks how she should in this house: nervous.

"I'm just here for my winter break," the new girl says quietly. "But I'm sorry about your mom."

"No, you're not," Margaret says with a little laugh. "Don't lie to me, whatever-your-name-is. How could you be sorry about someone you don't know? You're either stupid or you think that *I'm* stupid."

The girl is blinking at us in shock when a door slams open from somewhere in the front of the house. "Vanessa, come help me bring this stuff inside!" Miranda's voice echoes. Vanessa's face floods with relief at the sound, and she drops the peeler on the counter before disappearing into the hall without another word.

"Well," I say, looking at the food in my hands. "That was certainly something."

"It was like ripping off a bandage," Margaret says with a grin. "I can guarantee you that she won't bother us after this. Didn't want her to get the wrong idea, staying in a room so close to ours."

Glimpses like this, glimpses of the old Margaret, are what make my heart so desperate to believe that everything will be okay if I just wait it all out. *Just keep your back straight and deal with things as they come,* I tell myself. *Like Penelope would.*

"It sounds like Vanessa will only be here until the holiday party," I say, not enjoying the presence of another new person any more than my cousin is. "At least there's that." I frown at the idea of having the club here for dinner before then. The first one without Penelope will be especially strange.

"Yep, thank God," Margaret says, then raises the hand holding her waffle toward the glass patio doors leading to the courtyard. "I'm gonna eat this outside. You coming or what?"

I join her as she opens the sliding door and steps outside, where it's cold. The patio furniture is still wet from the rains last night, so we stand while we eat our waffles and sausage.

"Follow me," Margaret says after we've finished. She walks backward through the rows of dead rosebushes, her fingers extended and brushing roughly over the tips of the gnarled, thorn-laced branches. The damp chill in the air is biting. "Let's go for that walk."

"Where?" I say, following her with slight unease. There's something in her tone that's telling of a hidden agenda. She twirls around to face forward again. I notice a strange little skip in her step, an overly enthusiastic touch of pep that I don't think I've seen since we were seven.

"Tell me what's been going on with you." I rub my hands together in the cold, keeping my eye on her. "I'm kind of still worried."

"You should be, I think," Margaret says without turning her head, her voice serious. "I'm starting to worry about myself."

I knew it. She may have been acting more like herself this morning, but whatever was making her freak out before is still there. I wildly try to think of a way to ask her if she knows what happened to Penelope but can't find the courage to actually open my mouth about it. She'll only get mad, no matter what her answer is, and even if it was yes, it's not like that will make things better.

"I mean it," I finally manage as I follow her. She makes her way to the end of the courtyard. "We could tell my father that you need to talk to a doctor, and you could tell them all about the photos, or maybe what you thought you heard in the attic…"

She stops walking now. "You don't know what you're talking about, Lucy."

"Then help me understand," I try, but Margaret continues walking and doesn't say anything else. We cross over the end of the courtyard, into the dirt and rocks, when I realize that she's heading right for the forest where Penelope disappeared.

My heart jolts at the sight of the trees in the distance. I think about the last time I saw my aunt, how her raven braid lay against her back, how I saw her from the library window and wondered why she hadn't brought a coat or sweater with her for a walk that late in the afternoon.

"What are you doing?" I say, disturbed. "Is this supposed to be a joke?"

"You say you want to understand?" Margaret responds over her shoulder, meeting my eyes. "Then come with me."

"We have to go in *there*?" I stop walking. When she notices, she sighs loudly and puts her hands on her hips. What type of understanding could she possibly show me in the woods?

"Yes, Lucy," she answers, her impatience evident. "We have to go in there. Look, do you trust me or not?"

Do I trust Margaret anymore? It's hard to say after the past few days. Still, she looks at me now with hope, her eyes pleading with me that she doesn't want to do this alone. I realize as I look into her face, *just because she might know what happened to Penelope doesn't mean that she did it herself.*

"Of course I do," I say, deciding eventually that I mean it. Even through all the pain and all the acting out, it's still my best friend in there. *Even if she's not acting like much of a best friend anymore.* My confirmation of trust is all she needs to take her hands off her hips and continue on toward the trees.

"I feel really weird doing this," I call after her, but I'm not sure if she hears me or not. Before I know it, we're in the forest, stepping over dead branches and pinecones and brush. Margaret and I never really played around here as children because it was too far of a walk despite being part of the estate, and also the house itself was more than large enough to provide us with plenty of adventures in exploring. Still, Margaret walks as though she knows right where she's headed.

"Where exactly are we going?" I ask as I rush to follow my cousin. I can't believe we're here right now, the place I've been watching from afar for days, the place I've been fearing, the place that swallowed my aunt. What sorts of things could await us in here? My imagination is running wild.

"Lucy." Irritation laces her voice. "Stop acting like I'm leading you into a slaughterhouse."

"Don't you understand what we could find in here?" I demand, stepping gingerly over a pile of dead pine needles. "Why aren't you even a little bit unsettled right now?"

"Don't be such a baby," Margaret says with a tired half grin that pushes me too far. Screw this; it's going to turn into an attic situation all over again, ending with an argument way too far from home.

"I'm turning around," I say, just before I see something ahead, poking up through the dirt behind an especially dense cluster of trees.

"What is that?" Margaret asks, suddenly terrified, a complete turnaround from the moments leading up to this. "What the hell *is* that?" She's stopped walking midstride, staring at the thing, a strange-looking rock, perhaps? I don't understand why she's reacting so strongly to it.

"Calm down," I say, and this time it's my turn to feel smug. I make my way toward the stony thing, wondering why Margaret isn't leading the way or even following me.

The edges of the big rock ahead look too smooth, too shapely, to be made naturally . It seems to get larger with every step, an ever-expanding vessel of stone. I keep walking through the trees until I'm standing over it, my eyes wide, my brain struggling to understand what I'm seeing.

It's a tomb.

And, behind it, multiple scattered gravestones, each of them filthy and streaked with moss.

In all my time living here, I have never heard of there being a cemetery on the property. The estate has been in my family for generations, too, so I'm wondering if these are people I was related to in some way. I know my mother, grandmother and great-grandmother were all buried in one of the cemeteries in town, and these graves look *old*, so I doubt it.

There aren't words on any of the markers, or if there are, they are far too worn to distinguish. I step around the tomb and count twelve graves, all clustered together among the trees. There is no clearing, no gate, nothing at all to mark off the area of sporadically placed headstones of various sizes and shapes.

Margaret finally catches up to me after her hesitant

start, stepping out from behind an especially wide pine with caution.

"Weird, huh?" I say, watching her eyes take in the sight.

When my cousin sees the tomb and gravestones, she begins to scream.

SIX

SHE DOESN'T STOP screaming until I physically pull her away from the tomb. "What is wrong with you?" I yell over her cries as I lead her away.

Margaret quiets down after a step or two. I try to talk her into transitioning her quick, jagged gasps into slow, thoughtful breaths. I forcibly lead her through the trees, her panic fading as we get farther away from the graves. Her hands shake as she tightens her arm around mine, holding on and looking over her shoulder as if to make sure we aren't being followed.

"Margaret," I say, tears welling in my eyes. I don't care if she sees me cry; I can't handle it all anymore, the stress, the fear. Acosta or not, I am heading for a mental breakdown. "*Please* tell me what's going on. Please stop pushing me away because you're afraid, or angry, or whatever the hell it is. Let me be here for you!"

My cousin takes little gulps of air as she walks quickly with me in the direction that we came from. Once we've cleared the trees and the house is in sight, she lets go of my arm, shrugging away from me, walking toward the house as defiantly as she walked away from it less than an hour ago. *Something has to be done*, I realize right away. *I can't take this anymore.*

I have to tell my father about Margaret.

We go back inside through the double glass doors leading to the kitchen. Miranda and Vanessa are sitting at the wooden table in the corner, going over sheets of paper that look like they might be seating arrangement charts. Margaret goes through to the dining room exit without acknowledging their presence, and I tag along behind, returning Miranda's hesitant greeting with an empty smile and a hello. Vanessa looks flustered and miserable and pretends to be too engaged with whatever she's working on to look up. I wonder if she told her mom about what Margaret said.

I follow Margaret all the way to the main staircase in the parlor before I stop.

"Tell me what's going on with you," I say, giving it one last try. "Now. Because I'm about to go tell my father that you need serious help."

The grandfather clock in the entryway goes off, a whimsical melody followed by twelve long strikes that echo throughout all the open space of the room. When we were young, we'd always use this time to do something silly, like run screaming through the hallway or howl like a pack of wolves. If only life had a chance of resembling anything like that again, us giggling like lunatics while Penelope or my father bellowed up the stairs for us to settle down.

"Fine," Margaret says once the echo of the clock fades out. "But we need to wait until we're in your room. I don't want the stupid new girl to eavesdrop if we sit in here."

Yes. I nod gratefully and we go to the second floor. Once inside my bedroom, Margaret kicks off her shoes and sits on my bed, her arms wrapped around her middle.

"Sit down," she says softly, looking at the floor. "I need to say this stuff quickly or I'm not gonna end up saying it at all."

I sit on the floor at her feet so I can look up at her. "Tell me, Marg," I urge.

"Lucy..." she whispers, leaning down so that her mouth is closer to my ear. "I think I'm being haunted by my mom."

The warmth rushes from my hands, leaving them tingling. "What?"

"I've heard her say things...horrible things..." Margaret shivers and pulls a pillow onto her lap, hugs it tight. "It didn't start out bad. I went into the attic to hide from you and Uncle Felix after my mother was gone, and there was this knocking. It would mimic whatever I did."

She continues in a rush, using her remaining breath to say the rest in one long exhale. "It was almost like a *fun* thing, a friendly presence, and it was so nice not to feel alone, but then I started hearing her voice at night in my bedroom, telling me that I was going to end up in the same place she was..."

Her eyes well up with tears, a shockingly unfamiliar sight. All I can see in her face is suffering.

"Margaret." I wrap my arms around my knees, pull them close to my chest from where I sit on the floor. I speak purposefully slow, forcing calm. "You're not being haunted. You're grieving and sleep-deprived. You're not yourself."

"No," Margaret pleads, still whispering as if there's someone listening at the door. "It's not that, I swear it isn't. She's in the walls, Lucy. My mother's spirit is inside the walls and she's probably listening to us right now..."

"In the walls?" My heart skips a beat. "Think about what you're saying, Margaret. You need help, please let me help you..."

Margaret leans away from me when she sees my face. She looks down to her lap, wringing her hands around each other, curling her fingers into hooks. "I'm going to die," she says, not so much to me as herself. "My mom told me there was something waiting for me in the forest. A gift. She told me where to go, said that I'd know it when I saw it. She said I'd find my *future* there."

I remember the tomb and shudder. How did Margaret know where to find that graveyard, anyway? She must have known about it for a while and never mentioned it to me. Either way, what a breakdown she's plunging into. The question now: What happened to convince her that she's hearing things? I have to ask her if there's any hope of finding out.

"And my future is to be under the fucking ground," Margaret continues, nodding, her eyes moving slowly over my bedroom walls. "The only thing left to know is, who's gonna kill me?"

"Stop it," I say, crossing my arms over myself while I struggle not to yell. "You can't let yourself fall this deep. Whatever happened, you have to tell me about it, or the police if necessary, but either way you definitely need to see a doctor."

My cousin looks at me, her mouth slightly open in disbelief, as if she's been betrayed. "You really don't believe me. I told you what was happening and you don't believe me!"

"Do you know what happened to Penelope?" I ask bluntly, realizing that the window to do so is closing, and quick. Margaret's own words after we ran into Vanessa in the kitchen echo inside my head: *like ripping off a bandage.*

"Excuse me?" She stands quickly, and I instinctively flinch. "Oh, please," she snarls in reaction, walking past me to the door. "You really think I'm gonna snap and hurt you, Lucy? Do me a favor and try to do something that you've never been able to do in your entire life—get a grip."

And then she's gone.

The gravity of the situation settles over me, increasing my heart rate, making it hard to move, but I *must* move, and quickly at that. Margaret could be a danger to herself...or others.

She needs our help.

I peek out into the hallway to make sure the door to her bedroom is closed before heading downstairs. My father will almost certainly be in his study on the first floor, where he hides away for the length of most days, smoking cigar after cigar in his pressed suits and gel-slicked hair that's combed to the side while he goes over the books of the estate, as well as the schedules and lists for all the upcoming club activity.

I find him just like that, sitting at his desk, hunched over an open binder. When he sees me enter, he sits up straight, sets his pen down over the scatter of papers and takes a long draw of the cigar that's positioned on the edge of his nearly full glass ashtray.

"I need to talk to you," I say, watching the cigar smoke rise in swirling puffs above his head. "About Margaret."

"I'm listening." He turns his chair around to face the window so I can't see his face, which strikes me as especially rude.

"She's freaking out." I look nervously to the taxider-mied owl perched on the top of the bookcase. "Beyond what's reasonable, I'd say."

"You're talking about the photos in Penelope's room?" Another puff of smoke billows from behind the back of the leather office chair.

"No, not exactly," I say, taking a few steps farther into the room. "She thinks she's hearing a voice from inside the walls." Whose voice, I leave out—don't want to push any hot buttons too soon and miss out on any valuable information. "Did you know there's a ceme-tery on the property?"

He turns the chair now, relieving his cigar into the ashtray on the desk. "Yes, I did. Why?"

How did everyone know about this place but me?

"Why has nobody ever mentioned it?" I think back again to the tomb in the forest, and the gravestones that were green with moss. "And who's buried there? It re-ally freaked Margaret out, and then she told me about the voice in the walls. She seemed really sure, and she was acting like someone was going to kill her—"

"That's enough," my father says, frowning. "I don't have the energy for this."

"Welcome to my world!" I burst, no longer caring about being evasive. "Why haven't there been police over here since Penelope disappeared? Tell me the truth."

He's silent for a moment, then puts the cigar out and turns the chair back toward the window. "Lucy, I know that you miss your aunt very much. Please trust me when I say that I do, too." He doesn't sound choked up exactly, but there's something in his tone that indicates truth, longing even. "And trust me when I say that any and all appropriate measures were taken, including what was necessary regarding the police."

Before my aunt disappeared, the idea of her and my father being together was so strange. But at this point, I yearn so much for a reality where she is here, and okay, and they are happy together. Maybe cousins could have been sisters, after all. There's no way it could have possibly ended up being worse than what really happened.

"The way you've gone about things, your 'measures,' are pushing Margaret completely over the edge," I say. "Something needs to be done for her. She needs to see a therapist, somebody that'll help make sure she doesn't hurt herself…"

"She'll be fine," my father says, without emotion. "The little girl just needs to suck it up and get a hold of herself."

The cruelness of his words takes my breath away.

"No, you don't get it." I'm angry now, more than I

am scared. How could he say that? Does he not care about Margaret's well-being at all?

"I get it as much as I need to." My father pushes the ashtray aside, then picks up the pen he set down previously. "We're hosting a dinner for the club here in a few days, and organizing everything for it is killing me. Things are bad enough without Penny here to help—" He stops short when he realizes what he's done, revealed his nickname for my aunt without even meaning to. How can he hold her in such loving memory but dismiss Margaret without a second thought?

"Margaret has always been an especially dramatic child," my father continues. "Give her time, and she'll stop the destructive behavior."

So he's not going to do shit to help; he's just going to continue putting plans for a *dinner party* ahead of everything else? My thought circles back around to Margaret, of course. I wonder where she is right now, and what she's doing.

"Please close the door on your way out," my father says, which stings despite my will for it not to. He can never seem to get rid of me fast enough. "I've got a meeting with Miranda and a lot of paperwork to get through before the weekend is over."

"Whatever."

I slam the heavy door into its frame, creating a loud crash that echoes through the hall and all the way out to the entryway. In the massive silence of the parlor, I sit on a emerald velvet sofa that is positioned between a marble statue of an angel and an extra-tall houseplant. The chandelier that hangs from the vaulted ceiling glitters over my head.

I don't know whether to seek my cousin out or if doing so will only make things worse, push them further. She's probably in that attic right now, knocking on the walls and believing she can hear God knows what. *She's in the walls.* My cousin's words echo in my head, and I turn to look at the swirling gold-and-green Victorian wallpaper behind me.

I think about Margaret screaming when she saw the cemetery in the woods, and the desperation in her eyes when she first told me that she was being haunted. I think about how easily my father dismissed my concerns, how eager he was to get back to his work with his hobbies at the estate, his escape.

Or is it something else? I chew on my bottom lip as I remember Margaret's question about the police, how my father skirted around answering when I asked him just now, how my cousin remarked that we didn't know the real Penelope. Paranoia thickens the air around me, immobilizing me, and all I can do is sit on the emerald velvet couch and bite the skin on my lips as the grand chandelier of the entry room twinkles overhead.

When the clock strikes the next hour, I go into my bedroom to cut three neat little slashes into the flesh on my hip. As I wait for them to stop bleeding, I count all of my cuts, over and over and over again, until my heart stops beating in my ears and I can sit fully upright without wanting to sink the razor into my wrists and draw downward as hard as I possibly can.

SEVEN

I DON'T SEE Margaret until the night of the dinner party.

In our world, the world of trust funds and property estates and children who either go to private boarding schools or have paid tutors come to their homes, the reputation that is tied to your family's name means everything, especially within a hypersocial group like the country club.

Now that my mother and Penelope are both gone, my father has to work especially hard to uphold the family name. He is the one who changed his name to my mother's, *Acosta*, not the other way around. It was the Acostas who kept this historical estate in the family for generations, which is part of why Penelope was so angry when she wasn't the one to inherit, despite being the older sister. It was the Acostas who always kept to the top of the brutal socialite food chain, the most impressive family, the prettiest and wealthiest and most well involved. And now my father has inherited that burden, until it can be passed on to Margaret and me.

The evening of the party, when I'm done with my shower and am walking back to my bedroom, towel-wrapped and dripping onto the carpet, I hear my father bellow to Miranda from downstairs to use the plates with the real gold trim, not the china. After I step into my room and close the door, I go through my closet looking for a dress, wishing more than anything that I could pretend I was ill and skip out on this entire thing.

I wonder how Margaret is feeling tonight. She's been avoiding me since we got back from the woods, although the few times I've passed her in the hallways or the dining room she looked fine enough. No more dark circles, no more dirty clothes. I'm desperate to know if she still thinks she can hear Penelope in the walls. If she does, it's not like she's going to tell me about it. I'll need to keep an eye on her.

I take as long as I possibly can to get ready. By the time I'm finishing up on my hair, I can already hear the buzz of mass chatter coming from the usually silent downstairs area. I spray my pinned-up curls with hair spray, then carefully slip into my black party dress. A pair of matching pumps completes the outfit that feels much more like a uniform than anything else. When

I was little, I loved dressing up. Now it's just a hassle that happens all too often.

I'm about to head downstairs when I spot the bejeweled rose hair ornament on my vanity, just as beautiful as it's always been. It used to belong to Penelope, but after I kept asking to borrow it for events like this, she just gave in and let me have it, despite Margaret's hard expression as she watched from the doorway.

I stand over the vanity and run my fingertips over the ruby petals of the piece for a moment. I get that awful feeling in my stomach again, the feeling that Margaret knows something about Penelope's disappearance that she never told me. She never denied it when I asked her in my room; she only got defensive. I don't know what to believe anymore.

In the hallway, I can hear the sound of jazz playing from the record player in the dining room, hardly audible over the bursts of laughter and waves of voices all trying to talk over one another. I pause at the staircase, looking below to the sea of suits and fur shawls and hands holding glasses with cocktails or champagne. There appear to be about twenty of them in total: ten vainglorious men with their giggling, diamond-studded wives.

"Here comes our Lucy!" one of the more longtime members, Gregory Shaw, says as I step off the last stair and onto the polished floor. "Have a drink and chat with us, my dear!" Standing behind him is his wife, Nancy, the woman Margaret and I were mocking so ruthlessly earlier in the week. She really is the worst of them all.

Almost all of the furniture in the parlor has been removed or relocated against the walls, giving the already-spacious area a ballroom effect. Penelope always made sure it was set up this way for the dinner parties she orchestrated—my father must have filled Miranda in on what to do.

I think about how far he's willing to go to accommodate the club, to keep the Acosta name relevant. For the first time, I think about how that same pressure would have been all on Penelope before she disappeared. She always appeared to love it, but what if inside she was struggling? Desperation can make people do things that nobody would expect. The tender, still-healing skin on my hip is a raw testament to that.

"Hello." I smile and bow my head slightly in Gregory's direction, then give Nancy a little wave. "It's so wonderful to see you both again."

"Likewise, honey," Gregory says before taking a gulp of his martini. "I was a little surprised to hear that we were still on for tonight. Felix didn't have to go on with hosting if he didn't feel up to it."

I scan the room from where I stand, searching for Margaret. So far, no sign of her. I see Vanessa along the back wall, setting a tray of food onto a table with her back to me. She's gone out of her way to avoid me ever since that morning in the kitchen, which I am grateful for. It's like Margaret said: it's best that she knows to leave us alone.

"Well," I say, meeting Gregory's eyes again, "I think he probably liked having the distraction, to tell you the truth."

"So sorry to hear about your aunt, dear," Nancy says in a hushed voice, her lips painted bright with fuchsia. Her words are already starting to slur together from the gin in her nearly empty glass. "I truly adored her, such an Acosta she was, meticulous in every aspect of her life. This party isn't anything like the ones *she* used to throw." She pauses to take a sip from her drink, her eyes darting around the parlor to the snack table. "But I guess you can't hire that sort of perfection, can you, dear?"

"No, you can't," I say, forcing my smile to stay bright. "Of course, our family is still holding out hope regarding Penelope." It's a lie, but I know it's the right thing to say to keep up the reputation of the Acosta name. Any and all weaknesses are to be kept hidden out of sight.

"Of course you are," Gregory says, patting me on the shoulder. "As you should be. Nothing is ever certain, you know."

I'm surprised you feel that way, I feel compelled to say. *Especially since you were the first to stop coming to help search for her.*

I finally spot Margaret at the break in the staircase that leads to the second floor. She looks down at me, wearing a dress of rich jewel-toned blue that goes all the way down to the floor. There is a gold ribbon tied in her hair.

"Stop talking about Penelope," Nancy whispers drunkenly to her husband once she spots Margaret. "We don't want to upset her daughter, the poor thing."

Poor thing is right, I think sullenly as I watch my cousin descend the stairs. *If only they really knew.*

Margaret's smile is empty as she approaches. "Hello, everyone," she says after she's reached my side, nodding at Gregory and Nancy. "I sure hope dinner is ready soon, because I am starving."

"Me, too," Nancy says with a hiccup, emptying her glass of what little gin remains. "The food here was always divine, a perfect fit for an estate that's practically royal. You two are the luckiest girls in the world."

"No, we're not," Margaret says with unmistakable bite. "Both of our mothers are dead."

I feel myself blush in the awkward pause that follows. So much for holding out hope.

"I only meant that you live somewhere special, dear," Nancy replies drily, her eyebrow raised. "There's no need to get feisty. Historical landmarks like this are something to be respected."

My cousin frowns. "Respect, huh?"

"Excuse us," I say as politely as I can manage, then walk with Margaret to the food table, where we're alone. I watch as she inhales a tomato-sausage toast and two scallops straight from their shells. I want to ask her if she's all right, but I feel like that's one of the worst questions you could ask someone who just tried to convince you that she's hearing voices.

"So," I say after reaching for a tiny cup of puff pastry filled with avocado puree and spiced prawns. "How are you doing?"

"I'm okay," she says through her chewing. "Listen, I know I said some messed-up stuff before, about my mom, but I just wanted to say that I'm sorry for all that. I was…mistaken. Things are fine now, they really are."

"Mistaken?" I ask, hopeful. "So you're feeling better, then?"

"Yes," she says, offering up a weak smile. "I'm feeling better."

Miranda calls out from the entrance of the dining room that dinner is being served. The club members make their way across the parlor immediately, talking about the food and recent golf scores and each other.

"So no more voices?" I ask as we trail behind the crowd, daring to feel relief. "And no more attic?"

"No, she's still in there," Margaret says, and I close my eyes in pained disbelief. "I just said that I was mistaken. She doesn't want to hurt me. She just wants to *be* there for me. It's quite amazing, really, how she had to die for us to get so close."

I have to bite my lip to keep from screaming. We file into the dining room, finding our places marked with handwritten name cards. Margaret and I are placed together, as usual, but tonight I wish we weren't. *How does she know for sure that Penelope is dead?*

My father enters once everyone is seated, wearing a blue suit with a silver tie. He thanks everyone for coming, his voice artificially warm as he wishes a satisfying feast upon us all before sitting at the head of the table. The opposite head, where Penelope usually sits, remains empty. There is a black cloth draped over her chair.

"I want to say again how grateful I am for all the warm wishes and support you've provided in the wake of Penelope's disappearance," my father says, which is the easiest he's spoken of it in front of me yet. "Our family appreciates the help more than you could ever know."

"No thanks necessary, my friend," Gregory pipes up from where he sits across from me. "Your sister-in-law was one of the brightest and most outstanding members that this club has seen in years. Such potential she had. She will be sorely missed."

"Hear, hear," murmur random people from all around the table. A few members raise their glasses expectantly.

"To Penelope," Gregory speaks over my father. The rest of the drink glasses raise together in one swift movement. "May we always remember the grace she brought to this wonderful estate, her family birthright."

My father's eyes narrow, just in the slightest. Discomfort blooms in my belly, causing me to shift around in my seat. That mention about family birthright was a dig at my father, since he's only an Acosta by name. What idiot convinced everyone into thinking that kind of thing even matters? These are grown men in expensive suits and all they ever put into the world is pettiness.

Margaret's eyes are stuck on Gregory, her glass of sparkling cider raised, her eyes soft with affection at his words. I'm not surprised that she doesn't find the old man's comment to be inappropriate and disrespectful to my father. In fact, I'm sure she loves it. She'd love it even if she wasn't out of her mind right now.

The air becomes filled with the sounds of clinking glass, then long, thoughtful gulps. Margaret drains her glass before lowering it, which I find to be needlessly dramatic considering the toast. The fragrance of the platters upon platters of food before me calm my nerves. The featured dishes are clearly from Penelope's recipe book: lamb chops that have been seared and dusted with edible gold flakes, chickpeas and chorizo, whole roasted chickens and sea bass and blackened mackerel.

People begin serving themselves immediately, and the chatter goes on as though it never stopped. I watch as Margaret loads her plate up without turning to look at me once.

"We need to talk about this," I say to her under my breath, once I'm sure nobody is listening.

"No, we don't," her reply comes, quick and sharp. "It's clear to me that you aren't capable of understanding what's going on. I'm keeping this for myself."

I'm about to retort when a man named Kent Dickens, whom I've known just as long as I've known the Shaws, speaks up over the buzz of the crowd to address my father.

"Felix," he says through a horridly visible mouthful of sea bass. "What are your plans for the estate now that Penelope is gone?"

My stomach clenches in the same way that it did when Gregory gave his toast. Why must these people linger on things that are none of their business?

"My plans for the estate?" my father replies to Kent, his voice already on edge. "I plan to continue running it, of course. Penelope may have lived here and helped raise the girls, but I've been the one managing the immense responsibilities of this place since Eva passed away."

The murmur of chatter in the crowd dies down.

"I had no idea overseeing a staff was so difficult," Kent says in a lighthearted tone. "Still, I meant no offense by the question, Felix."

Sure he didn't. Kent's wife, Mary-Anne, a dark-haired lady with impressively smooth skin for her age, looks deeply embarrassed as she scoops more chorizo onto her plate.

"Of course not," Gregory pipes in. "I'm sure Kent just meant that it must feel strange being the king of a place where you have no authentic blood roots—"

"The Acosta name will carry on," my father interrupts. "As I'm sure you remember, I had my name changed when Eva and I married, and my daughter, Lucy, was born into it, as well. I've always been fully aware of the connection this place has to the club. I will continue to provide the space for get-togethers and galas, I will continue to fund whatever is needed for our projects of interest..."

"Well now, Felix," Gregory cuts in. "There's no need to get defensive, my boy. I have never been less than impressed with your contributions to our club and the community of Scarborough Falls."

My father doesn't respond, instead draining the sangria from his glass before pouring more.

"Let's move on," I say loudly, much to the shock of Kent and Gregory. If they won't respect my father for his lack of "authentic" Acosta blood, I will drown them out using mine. "What a thing to bring up in front of everybody at the first gathering without my aunt. And from someone who just made a toast in her honor, no less."

Embarrassed silence from Gregory and Kent; supportive nods from other members. My father nods at me ever so slightly, but I don't return the gesture. I didn't do it for him, I did it for Penelope. And myself, to be honest, because if I had to listen to one more second of it all, I would have screamed.

"Good job, sweetie," Nancy slurs to me from across the table. "Something tells me that your aunt would have been extremely proud to see you defuse a nonsensical situation such as that."

Margaret lets out a sharp little sigh from beside me. If Gregory hears his wife's words, he doesn't show it, instead carrying on with someone sitting to Margaret's left about the current state governor. Nancy goes on stuffing her face with food and guzzling her drink, and the rest of the meal goes on without incident.

After dessert has been served and consumed, the couples leave one by one, all stopping to say goodbye or give condolences before they disappear into the night, except for Gregory and Kent, who slip out quietly with their wives when my father isn't looking.

Once everybody's gone and the house is silent again, my father goes into the kitchen to make sure Miranda and Vanessa are ready to pack away the leftover food and clean up, then returns to the dining room to announce he is turning in early.

"Thank you for what you said earlier," he mumbles as he passes me, his hands stuffed awkwardly into his pockets. "Gregory has always been envious of this estate, and it doesn't help any that he was rejected by

Penelope decades ago and had to marry that horrible Nancy woman…"

"It's all right," I say, unable to resist smiling just a little bit at the visual of Penelope shooting Gregory down. I never heard that before. I wonder if Nancy knows. "He was totally out of line."

"You're making that up," Margaret scoffs from where she stands beside me in the entry room, at the foot of the grand staircase. It's the first time she's spoken since dinner. "Gregory is nicer than I've been giving him credit for. It's his wife who's out of line. Mom would have been lucky to be with a man like him. She never would have turned him down."

My father laughs darkly. "Believe what you want to believe," he says as he disappears into the unlit hallway that leads to his study. "Good night, girls."

"Good night," I call after him.

"Your dad is delusional," Margaret says with a huff and turns to head up the stairs. "He's just mad that she didn't love *him*."

But she did love him, and I'm pretty sure my cousin knows it deep down. Let her continue to deny it; it's not like it matters anymore, anyway.

"Wait," I say. "You shouldn't be alone right now. Just come hang out in my room tonight. We can talk, or—"

"It's too late for that shit," she replies without a

pause. "By the way, how does it feel to know that you're not Penelope's favorite anymore?"

My heart skips in my chest. "Margaret," I say as calmly as possible. "You've lost your mind. How do you not realize it? A few days ago you said Penelope's ghost was in the walls, that she wanted you dead. Now you're closer than you've ever been?"

"She heard us talking the other day in your room." Margaret is still making her way up the stairs. "After we found those graves. She said I misunderstood, and she explained things to me, she even talked about *you*—"

"Christ, Margaret!" I cut her off. "What is *happening* here?"

She does pause then, midway to the second floor. "Why don't you tell me?"

I stare at her, trying to figure out if I believe she is capable of hurting my aunt.

"You had a bad relationship with Penelope, and now she's gone," I say, no longer wanting to hold back, wondering instead if I can make her confess something. "You're obsessing over it, and you're taking it out on me because she and I were so close, but you *know* something, Margaret. You know something that you haven't told me!"

"You are so self-centered." Margaret laughs. "I saw the way you used to puff your chest out after my mom would compliment you on anything. Well, guess what, cousin? She only treated you that way because she felt sorry for you. Because your dead mom was a bitch and your dad is so pathetic that he could hardly keep it in his pants whenever he was around his own sister-in-law."

My face gets hot, and I take a step toward her. Hard times for Margaret or not, I'm pissed. "How dare you?"

"And you wonder why I don't talk to you about stuff anymore," she says, coming down just one step as she glares. "You're so judgmental. I know things about you, you know, things my mom told me in the attic the other night, things that you'd be humiliated to know were no longer secret."

"You need to be committed," I say in all seriousness. "I'll make the call myself if I have to, first thing in the morning."

"You'd better leave me alone, Lucy," Margaret says over her shoulder as she heads past the break to the second floor and onward to the third. *Going to the attic again. Of course.*

"Or else what?" I call up the stairs.

"I'll tell your father all about that sick little box you keep in your room."

I freeze where I stand, willing myself not to show any reaction. "What?"

"Do you realize how profoundly fucked up it is that you've *decorated* that thing?" she continues. "Something tells me there's more evidence in this house to put you away than there is for me."

For a second I feel like I might throw up. She wouldn't do that, would she? What would my father say? A lump forms in my throat at the realization that I actually care about what he thinks about me. It's something I've vehemently denied to myself over the past years in reaction to how cold he is, to me, to Margaret, to everybody except Penelope. But I don't *want* to care what he thinks; why can't I just change that? Of all the things I've kept under control, why can't I have that one thing?

Now, seeing the look on Margaret's face, I believe that she would tell.

I remember how I felt to wake up to the scissors pointed at my throat, how her fist was shaking, like she was having to stop herself from killing me right then and there. "What's happened to you?" I finally manage.

"Something that should have happened a long time ago," she calls down from the top of the grand staircase before heading down the dark hallway that leads to the attic. "I finally got my mother back."

EIGHT

I ARRANGE PIECES of wood inside the fireplace in my bedroom as soon as I get in, my movements rigid and slow. I regret nothing in my life as much as I regret showing Margaret my collection of razors and lighters and pins—how could I have ever thought it was a good idea?

Because she was your best friend, I think. *Because you were tired of feeling alone. Because you shouldn't have had to worry that she'd use it against you someday.*

But she is, and I am helpless to the threat. How did I fail to notice that telling Margaret my secret would give her all the power over me? I showed her my ultimate weakness. Shame burns hotter than anything else inside me, rising, all-encompassing. The idea of that shame being exposed to my father and the world is enough to immobilize me.

I refuse to even look at the cigar box on my vanity shelf, the jewels and glitter shimmering in the light of the fireplace. I don't just feel the weight of my inevitable loss of control to it—now there's humiliation, too. I thought I was so strong when I first started using the razors and pins, a true Acosta making her own way, but in truth I've been weak from the start. And Margaret? I'm starting to believe she's more than just reckless. I'm starting to believe that she's dangerous, too.

After getting into bed, I hold my hands over my ears, blocking out the nonexistent sounds of the box pleading with me to come take a peek inside, to come find some relief in the pain.

Think about something else, I command myself desperately. So instead of the razors, I think about what Margaret said when she got upset in my bedroom a few days back, about her future being under the ground. I'm starting to believe that mine might be, too.

Maybe then, *finally,* I won't have to be alone anymore. Or if I am, I most certainly won't give a shit. Either way, I win. After a few more minutes of lingering on the fantasy of eternal peace, I am able to lower my hands from my ears. I eventually climb out of bed to change into loose cotton pajamas and wipe off my makeup, before returning. I wiggle in between the two pillows and pull the duvet and satin sheets up to my chin, forming a protective cocoon.

The darkness of my bedroom comforts me, as it always has. Margaret is afraid of the dark, oddly enough, even with her fireplace lit. She hates how the flames cause strange shadows to flicker over the walls. She used to say it made it look like the swirl design of the elaborate Victorian wallpaper was curling into itself.

But it's that same atmosphere that helps me feel hidden, quiet, calm. As long as I'm in here, everything is okay, at least for now. My door is locked and it's late enough to go to sleep.

Tomorrow will be even worse than today, I say to myself in warning, to begin the mental preparation now. I remember the hatred in Margaret's eyes at the end of our fight, when she called me judgmental, and the great sadness deep inside me flexes its brawny muscle again, still sore from when I fantasized about death. I find myself terrified of what awaits me in the daylight.

There comes a gentle knock on the door. I sit up, confused as to why the fire is almost out already. Did I fall asleep without realizing it? I get up in the near-dark and make my way to the door. Standing in the hallway is Vanessa, looking tired and unhappy.

"I'm sorry if I woke you up," she says, not sounding sorry at all. "But is there any chance you know where Margaret is? She's not in her room and I thought she might be in here."

"Why are you looking for her?" I lean against the door frame, still woozy from sleep, eager to get back to bed. "She's probably up in the attic again, on the next floor up."

Vanessa nods and walks away without another word, her ponytail swaying behind her.

"Wait," I call after her when I process what just happened, suddenly feeling very awake. "Why are you trying to find Margaret this late?"

Vanessa doesn't answer, just loops the corner of the hallway and disappears. I run after her, fast enough to catch up by the time she's made it to the staircase. I wasn't thinking when I told Vanessa about the attic.

"Stop," I say, and the girl turns to stare at me impatiently. "She's not feeling very well and it would be a bad idea to interrupt her while she's up there."

"I don't really care how she's feeling," Vanessa says, her face flushed from walking so quickly. "She's going to come downstairs to clean up the mess she made and apologize to my mother, or I'm going to call the police."

"What are you talking about?" I ask, my stomach dropping. "What did she do to Miranda?"

"As if you don't know," Vanessa says, narrowing her eyes. "My mom swears up and down that it had to have been Margaret alone, that *she's* the troubled one, but I've seen how you two are together, so forgive me for jumping to conclusions. Because if you don't mind me saying, you and your cousin both seem kind of fucked up."

The girl's glare is cutting. I can't tell her she's wrong, because she isn't.

"What did she do?" I ask, out of my mind worried about whatever the answer will be. "Tell me what she did and I'll go with you to find her."

Vanessa's eyebrows relax, her mouth still turned down. "You really have no idea?"

"No."

The new girl sighs and looks up to the darkened third floor. "She left a dead rat on my mother's pillow. Cut open. Its guts were spread out all over the pillowcase."

I raise a hand to cover my mouth, wishing I hadn't answered my door. I thought I was scared before, but this is a nightmare come to life.

"My mom walked in on her and she bolted," Vanessa continues. "I showed up a few minutes later to say good-night and she told me what happened. Now I'm here."

"Oh my God." I feel ill.

It's never going to stop escalating, I realize. She's snapped, and there's no going back. Even if it ends with me getting sent away, I need to get her some outside help and end this. I have no idea what will happen to me, but after what I've just heard, I'm beyond caring. Let me take down the family's reputation single-handedly. Let my father find out who I really am.

Let me prove to myself that I'm capable of being strong, just once.

"I'm so sorry," I say to Vanessa, scared at what else my cousin might do.

"I don't want to hear that from you," she says, continuing to go up the stairs to the third floor. "I want to hear it from her. Right after she finishes explaining to me why she'd do such a fucked-up thing to someone who busts her ass to keep this ridiculous freak show up and running."

I imagine how the dinner party with the club must have looked to someone who wasn't born into it. *Freak show* comes pretty close, I guess.

"I realize you're really mad," I say, scrambling to follow her. "But I don't think confronting her about it here and now is a good idea, seriously. She's messed up about her mom. She's not right in the head." I need to get rid of this girl, and fast.

"I'm going to talk to her about it," she says, "and I'm going to talk to her about it now."

I'm beginning to panic. There is no possible way this will end even close to okay. "Just let me go in first," I plead, trying to stay close to Vanessa as she reaches the top of the stairs. "To give her a heads-up so she doesn't get too startled. Trust me when I say that it's for your own good, seriously!"

She finally slows her pace, then stops to look back at me.

"Fine," she finally agrees, crossing her arms. "Hurry up, please."

At least there's that. I nervously make my way down the hallway that leads to the back corner of the house, my pulse still pounding in my ears from Vanessa's confrontation. I need to do what I can to make sure that this doesn't turn into a full-on brawl between the two of them, and get Margaret to my father immediately. But when we finally turn toward the back corner of the third floor, the sight is unexpected.

The miniature staircase descending from the attic opening is shrouded in shadow.

The light in the attic is off.

"Are you sure she's up there?" Vanessa whispers, sounding uneasy. "You do realize what time it is, right? Why would she be up there in the dark?"

Margaret's afraid of the dark.

"She's been sleeping up there," I respond. I feel jittery at the idea of climbing up into the dark space and turning on the light. "I told you, she isn't right in the head."

"I figured that out the first time I met her," Vanessa says. For a moment I'm embarrassed about what she said. *You and your cousin both seem kind of fucked up.* After the past few days, I can't even bring myself to disagree with her, and that's the worst part. Who have I become?

I climb the tiny steps up into the pitch-black. The air in the attic is cool against my hot face. I don't hear anything, not Margaret snoring, not Margaret breathing. I wave my hand wildly in front of myself, trying to locate the chain that hangs from the single bulb somewhere in the center of the room. I inch forward, dragging my feet to avoid stepping on my cousin if she's sleeping on the floor.

"Are you guys screwing with me?" I hear Vanessa's voice below me. "Why aren't you turning on the light?"

I'm trying, I want to say, but don't want to startle Margaret awake. I hurry my pace, and my fingers finally graze across the cold metal string hanging in the air in front of me. I pull it down hard and quick, gasping as all my pent-up fear releases and the room is flooded with light.

The attic is empty.

"Hello?" Vanessa calls up again. "Can I come up now?"

"She's not here," I say, goose bumps flourishing over my arms. I climb back down through the opening on the floor, not bothering to turn the light off. "You said you looked in her room?"

"Yes." Vanessa looks let down at Margaret's absence. "She's probably off mutilating another animal or something. Sicko."

I take off for the stairs again. Where else would she be at this time of night? *Something is wrong*, my brain screams, and my head gets light with anxiety.

"Maybe she's hiding in one of these extra rooms," Vanessa says, taking in the amount of closed doors studded along the hallways.

"Maybe," I say, even though I know for a fact that she's not. If my cousin was hiding, it'd be somewhere good, undetectable and most definitely not a guest bedroom. Regardless, I can no longer put on a front for this girl. "Why don't you check them out while I try her room again?"

She nods seriously and walks into the first spare room, turning the light on as I head for the stairs. I need to talk to Margaret alone first, before the new girl goes crazy on her and possibly sets her off, and before I take her to my dad. But where is she?

I go briskly back down to the second floor, opening my cousin's door just long enough to confirm that her room is indeed empty. I decide to check the library next, since it's on the same floor and was frequented by Margaret somewhat often before Penelope disappeared. After looping around the horseshoe-shaped hallway, I step into the library.

I don't even bother to turn on a light—it's not necessary with the amount of moonlight that is streaming in through the massive wall of windows in the back. I call my cousin's name and weave my way through the shelves of books, which tower over me in the shadows. I try not to imagine Margaret's hand shooting out from behind one of the shelves, still holding the knife she used to cut open the rat, the blade slicing through my Achilles tendon like butter. Soon, I've searched through the entire room and find myself at the chair

I moved in front of the window to overlook the forest days before. The sight of the chair makes me want to throw it through the glass.

I'm about to head out to scour the first floor when I see something through the window that catches my eye, off in the distance where the forest begins.

The glow of a flashlight.

Someone is returning from a walk in the woods. As I squint out the window, I notice that whoever is holding the flashlight isn't just walking, they're running. I watch, breathless, as the light gets closer and closer to the house. I see that it's heading toward the entrance in the kitchen, and I bolt out of the library and down the stairs. I'm halfway through the dining room when Margaret steps in from the kitchen, still holding the flashlight.

"Hi!" she manages, completely out of breath. "I'm glad you're here, Lucy."

My blood runs cold as I take in my cousin's outfit: a pair of blue pajama bottoms and a loose, black tank top. There is blood all over her hands. *She really did cut open a rat!* I search her free hand for a knife but don't see it. *She could be hiding it in her waistband.*

"Margaret," I say, struggling to sound calm. "Why were you outside this late, and why didn't you bring a coat? It's freezing outside."

"I don't care," she says, giggling a little. Without warning, she rushes forward, causing me to startle and step back. She runs past me, going straight for the stairs, and I run after her.

"Did you put a dead rat on Miranda's pillow?" I ask, my heart still beating erratically at the idea of Margaret walking in the forest alone at night. "Her daughter wants to kick your ass, Margaret. She's upstairs looking for you right now."

Margaret bursts out laughing in response, the sound echoing off the walls of the entry room. I cringe, wondering if my father is going to be awakened by the commotion. I really wanted to talk to her alone before he was brought into all of this.

"Where are you going?" I ask, already knowing that the answer is the attic.

"To talk to my mom." She turns back to look at me, her eyes alive with joy. "I went back to that cemetery, you know. The one that my mom said was my future. It's not that scary anymore. In fact, it's not scary at all. We can't *fear* the future, Lucy. The only thing we can do is prepare for it. Get excited for it. Greet it with open arms. Share it with others."

I almost become dizzy by the amount of concern that floods through my body. "What do you mean, Margaret?" I ask as I hurry to keep up. "Please stay out of the attic. This has gone far enough. You need help. Let's go call somebody right now, please, Margaret, *please...*"

But we've already reached the third floor, and my

cousin is bolting into the hallway leading to the back corner. "Wait!" I yell and see Vanessa step out of one of the spare rooms, her face confused.

"Did you find her?" she asks as I go by. She looks ahead of me and spots Margaret. "Hey, there you are! We need to talk about some things, you and I."

"Screw off," my cousin replies as she hurries up the miniature staircase leading to the attic. Vanessa's eyes come alive with anger, like they were before.

"Look," I say to Vanessa, still standing in the hallway, every passing second a great sacrifice. "I'm not kidding. You need to leave her alone right now. Something's wrong." I don't know what else to say to make her go away.

She doesn't answer me, just looks at me like she's trying to figure out what to do, but I don't have time to wait. I climb up after Margaret, and the new girl follows me. By the time I step into the room, Margaret is standing with her back against the same wall she was knocking on when she first brought me up here, struggling to catch her breath. The air is much colder than it was when I came to look for her not fifteen minutes ago.

"I love my mother so much," Margaret says with a smile, just as Vanessa climbs into the attic, as well. "I never understood her when she was alive. When she first came back to me, I was afraid, but now I understand. I understand everything. She's here with us, right now."

"What is she talking about?" Vanessa asks nervously. She looks a lot less angry and a lot more uneasy now.

"There's a way I can see her again," my cousin continues, ignoring Vanessa, only looking at me. "And everything will be fine."

"Vanessa," I say, my voice cracking. "Please go downstairs and wake up my father."

"Okay," Vanessa agrees instantly, backing toward the opening in the floor before disappearing through it. I wait until she's gone to speak.

"Margaret." I offer my cousin an attempted smile and take a step forward. "Everything *is* fine, just come here..."

"I can't," she says, pointing behind me. "There's something I have to do first."

I turn quickly, noticing for the first time that the large circular window on the wall across from the one Margaret is leaning against is wide-open, the carved wooden covering pulled back, the night sky exposed. That's why it's colder in here than it was before. I'm about to ask my cousin why she opened the window when I realize that the screen is missing, like it's been pushed out.

"No!" I scream too late, at the same time Margaret rushes by me in a blur of blue pajama pants and dark hair. I reach out to grab the back of her shirt but just miss her. As I watch, my cousin rushes to the open window, steps up onto the circular frame and jumps out.

I scream again, sprinting to the window, looking out despite the dreadful knowledge that I will regret doing so.

And I do. Instantly.

Because after my cousin falls three stories, she lands directly on top of the spiked iron fence that runs along the perimeter of the garden. I watch as two black metal spikes explode through the back of her shoulder and head, the impact causing pieces of bone and brain matter to go in every direction. Her arms and legs flail weakly, like she's a dying insect, and even from all the way up here I can hear the sound of her gurgling whimpers before the nerves die out and she finally goes limp. Blood pours from her body, runs down the fence, pools over the cobblestone, sinks into the grass.

When my father and Vanessa climb up into the attic and pull me away from the gaping mouth in the wall, I'm still screaming Margaret's name.

NINE

IN MY FAVORITE photograph of Penelope, she is standing in the garden, just in front of the ivy-covered stone wall outside the house, her arm draped around a ten-year-old me. We're both wearing sun hats and gardening gloves and ridiculous smiles. At our feet are baskets of freshly harvested tomatoes and squash and herbs, our summer bounty, surrounded by piles of long-stemmed flowers that we sorted according to color. My aunt's free hand is frozen in midair, waving to whoever took the picture, my father, most likely. The ends of her dark, curly hair are pulled sideways from the breeze.

Her face is scribbled out with black ink.

It is in all the photos now. Margaret got to each and every one somehow, one of the many warning signs that should have prompted me to ensure her safety sooner than I did. The photographs, her reaction when we first discovered the cemetery, her claim that Penelope's ghost was trapped inside the walls of the house.

What was it my father said when I confronted him about Margaret in his study? *The little girl just needs to suck it up and get a hold of herself.* Of course. Because little girls never worry about anything important enough to require more than a second's thought, apparently.

I failed you, Margaret.

We failed you.

Now I'll never get to see her again, never get to talk things out, or make them right. The knowledge that she loved me isn't what I seek; I know she did, and she knew I loved her just as much. It's the state of how things were between us that tortures me now, so many things unspoken in the wake of Penelope's disappearance, so many lost chances to say something sooner and save her, somehow.

In the entire length of our history together, never once despite her moodiness and sharp tongue did Margaret ever appear to fall completely out of touch with reality. At first I thought her recent bout of strange behavior spawned from the shock, or grief, or maybe even regret from how horrible things were between her and her mother. I thought it would pass.

And now she's dead.

The ever-growing black hole of grief and loss that never had the chance to develop from my mother's absence has erupted into existence overnight. I've gone from having my aunt and cousin to having nei ther in less than a month. For the first time in my life, I'm acutely aware that my own mother is gone. In fact, I can't seem to forget it no matter how hard I try.

How would things have gone if she never had the brain aneurysm? What kind of person would I be today? Different? Better? Would Margaret and Penelope have been better off living in their tiny apartment in town, bitter about being left out of the will, rather than changing their lives to revolve around me and my father and the club?

Likely, yes. Running through all the potential possibilities is driving me mad, but it's still better than focusing on what's real in my life now: Margaret is gone forever.

I'm a different person now, I realize as I get back into my bed, the satin sheets as cool as the air in the attic was. The fireplace in my bedroom glows red from the dying embers piled over the stone. I don't even know who I am without my cousin.

Is her body still out there? I wonder as I pull the covers up to my chin, my eyes open and staring, unblinking, up at the ceiling. I think about the sound her head made when the tip of the black iron fence exploded through the back of it. *Would my father have taken her down from the fence while he waited for officials to arrive?*

What *officials* he called remains to be seen. Who

do you call for something like this? A paramedic? An undertaker? I wonder if Vanessa is still awake, if she's told her mother about Margaret yet, how Miranda took the news. My father insisted that I go back to bed while he took care of things. I hardly even remember climbing down out of the attic, or making my way back to my bedroom on the second floor. Somewhere in between I stopped to wash my face and hands with scalding water.

I can practically feel the emptiness of Margaret's bedroom behind the wall my bed is pushed up against. Tomorrow I should go through her things, take everything I could possibly want before my father hires someone to clear it away and donate it all. I wonder if he feels guilty for ignoring what I told him about Margaret. I hope so.

After a few deep breaths, I finally gather the courage to close my eyes. I struggle to keep my brain from replaying the events of the night, and the events leading up to it, and the vision of Margaret becoming impaled on the fence with her blood pouring all over the cobblestone and the grass.

Just a handful of hours ago we were in fancy dresses, eating roast chicken and listening to stupid Gregory Shaw lay into my father about his future with the estate. How did things take a turn so quickly?

Margaret told me that Penelope had *explained* things to her about the cemetery in the forest, the same one she went to tonight before she killed herself. When she first saw the place, she freaked out, but this time she had gone all by herself in the middle of the night? It doesn't make any sense. She must have already lost herself to whatever sickness had awakened in her mind.

I remember hearing the sound of Margaret through the wall, crying in her room late at night before things went from bad to worse. And how she cried again when she tried to tell me what was going on with her. More clues I should have taken to heart: she never cried.

I can almost hear the crying now. In fact, uncomfortably so.

Impossible, I think to myself without opening my eyes. *She's dead. That's not her crying you hear, it's just your own messed-up mind remembering the memory too vividly...*

But I do hear it—the sound of Margaret crying in the other room. I must be asleep; there are no ghosts, no matter how much my cousin may have believed otherwise. She was so sure she could hear Penelope, or maybe she just needed to believe it.

But then I remember something that's been bothering me.

That first time Margaret and I went to the woods— she walked through the forest as though she knew exactly where she was going. How had she known where to go like that? At the time I figured she must have been there before, but then I saw how she'd reacted when we reached the tomb. She clearly was

not expecting those graves. Who had told her where
to go?

Certainly not a ghost, I think in an attempt to calm
my nerves. *There's a valid explanation here, you just don't
know it.*

*Just like there has to be a valid explanation for the crying
you can hear now, right?*

I don't open my eyes to see if I am dreaming or not.
To do so would mean that I'm entertaining the idea
that something unnatural is happening. I need to stop
thinking, stop dreading tomorrow, stop dreading the
rest of my life, however long that may be. I need the
memory of Margaret running past me to get to the
window, her hair flying behind her, still smelling of
pine from the forest, to stop replaying in my head.

I read once that scientists don't really know why we
physically require sleep besides the fact that we just get
tired. I'm starting to believe that we simply wouldn't
be able to *survive* if we weren't able to turn off for
hours at a time, the screen black, our bodies nothing
more than idling vehicles released from the weight of
simply living.

I have the same dream all night, a nightmare in
which I can hear Margaret's voice chiding me in the
dark of my bedroom. "How could you do this to me?"
she weeps from under my bed, her cries muffled as

though she's somehow pressing her face against the bottom of the mattress. "How could you let me die even after I asked for help?"

TEN

I SLEEP FOR nearly two full days, only leaving the warmth of the blankets when I have to get up and use the restroom. Nobody comes to bother me. I'm glad that my father knows to stay away. I haven't heard any sounds to indicate that Margaret's bedroom was being cleaned out, either.

Eventually, the bed stops comforting me and starts suffocating me, with its sheets clinging to my clammy skin and tangling themselves around the bottoms of my ankles like hands. I try to kick them off, grunting in frustration when I only succeed in tangling them further.

When I stand, I feel thick in the head. The aftermath of witnessing Margaret's death has settled into my body like an especially wicked hangover. The temperature is near frigid, as I haven't been keeping up with my fireplace. I walk in a big circle around my room, hugging myself as I carefully take in what everything looks like in this strange new world I live in, the world without Penelope *or* Margaret.

Out the window, the sun is blocked by a thick array of dark gray clouds. I step up to the glass and glance sharply to the right, where I can see the black iron fence that surrounds the garden. My cousin's body is gone. The cobblestone and fence have been cleaned of her blood, and the patch of grass that was puddled with it has been cut out, the dark soil striking against the green.

I wonder where her body is, and when the funeral will be.

I shiver as I turn away from the window and get myself dressed as quickly as possible. Afterward, I make my way through the empty dining room and into the kitchen to grab something from the bread shelf for breakfast. I don't see any sign of Miranda or Vanessa anywhere and wonder briefly if it's possible that they quit, or if Vanessa did, at least. The girl thought my cousin and I were fucked up *before* one of us babbled about a ghost and killed herself.

The thought is only a dismal reminder that I have no idea why Margaret did what she did. The circumstances are too extreme to let them be swept under the rug, which I know is the direction my father will go as far as moving on from this. Something strange is happening and there has to be an answer, or at least part of one, somewhere. She was keeping a secret; maybe I can find out what it was. I can look through her bedroom, maybe even Penelope's. I could put my mind to use instead of having it run in constant, violent circles.

As I'm leaving the kitchen, I see papers spread out over the small table in the corner—more seating arrangements for an event that is supposedly a week away, according to the date scribbled in the corner. Margaret's memorial, perhaps? I would have thought that over a week is a long time to wait for funeral and memorial services—too long—but maybe I'm mistaken.

After some thought, I decide to go to Penelope's room, which I've been avoiding for weeks. The idea of going into Margaret's room first fills me with a cold, electric fear, a deeply threaded string of dread that feels as though it's sewing my heart closed stitch by stitch. Penelope's door is closed but not locked, which I half expected after my father discovered what Margaret had done to the pictures. I slip in and close the door behind me before taking in the sight of Penelope's room.

Her bed is made, and there are small piles of clothing scattered over the hardwood floor. A framed painting of a rabbit hangs crookedly over the swirling wallpaper. Scarves lie in piles over the dresser. Overcome, I lie facedown on her bed, inhaling the familiar scents of lavender and cigarette smoke.

What happened to you, Penelope? And what did Margaret know about it?

After I've taken a moment, I go to my aunt's large wooden dresser that sits against the wall by the entrance to her bathroom. Margaret always used to remark how stupid it was that Penelope loaded her dresser drawers with pictures and trinkets and books as opposed to clothes, but I thought it was wonderful, having your most precious items all stored together somewhere that is organized and accessible.

The bottom drawer is books: fiction, old Spanish cookbooks that belonged to her grandmother, hard-cover notebooks filled with drawings she did of different parts of the house. I flip through the notebooks, aching with sentiment as I take in the lazy sketches of the entry room and the courtyard and the garden. Penelope was always so deeply in love with this house, with its historical architecture and wide-open spaces. She couldn't get enough of it, even referred to the grounds as sacred from time to time.

I am filled with relief to discover that Margaret didn't wreck any of these notebooks, but the nostalgic half smile blooming on my face fades away when I look into the middle drawer, the one with all of Penelope's photographs. Every single one is ruined, just as my father said they were, but seeing it with my own eyes just makes it more appalling.

One photo shows Penelope at a country club summer picnic that took place in the courtyard, her head held high and proud as she stands in a yellow house-

dress among the rosebushes and the guests. The word
BITCH is scrawled sloppily across the entire sky. Penelope's face is covered in scribbles, as are her feet and
the single rose that is being extended to her by a man
in a blue suit, Gregory Shaw. The sight of it is eerie
enough to make me feel ill.

I go through the piles and piles of defiled photos,
each one containing more scribbles and curse words
than the last. I try to imagine Margaret coming in
here, grim-faced and equipped with a black marker.
No matter how hard I try, I can't figure out what her
intentions were at that moment; whom she was trying
to hurt by ruining the photos. Her mother? My father?
Me?

The next photo was taken on my seventh birthday
and shows Penelope setting a cake down before me,
her mouth open in silent song. The flame of each candle has been crossed out, and long, jagged teeth have
been drawn over my aunt's mouth, monster-like. Instead of scribbles like she did every other time, Margaret had very carefully outlined and filled my face in
with solid black ink.

Clearly, my cousin's jealousy about my relationship with Penelope wasn't something I'd made up or
even exaggerated in my head. But what was it that
made her so especially angry with Penelope, enough
to come in here and do something like this to all of
her memories?

You don't know the first thing about my mother, Margaret said that night at dinner when my father first questioned her about the photos. *Neither of you do, and that's the problem.*

I drop the photos back into the dresser drawer in disgust, then slide it shut. I've seen enough. I give the rest of the room a quick look-over, and even though the sight of her purse and car keys hanging on the coatrack by the door hurts bad enough to make me cringe, I don't find anything unusual or out of place. I take one last longing look around my aunt's bedroom, wondering how she would have felt over what happened to Margaret, then open the door to step out.

My father is standing in the hallway.

His suit is impeccable as always, the cuff links silver today, his hair combed to the side with a swath of hair gel. The intensity of his stare is startling.

"Hi," I say, pulling the door shut behind me as I step into the hall. "I was just thinking of Penelope and I thought I'd—"

"How are you feeling?" he cuts in, sliding his hands into his pockets. "You were pretty quiet for a few days there. I was beginning to get worried."

"Huh?" I ask, taken by surprise at the concern. "Yeah, I think I'll be okay. It's just...what happened with Margaret was..."

I remember my father pulling me away from the attic window, screaming, and blush.

He looks to the floor, frowning. "Yes. I am so sorry you had to witness that. It's a shame that she took such drastic measures to make her statement. We're all hurting, even more so now."

Her *statement*? Any warmth his concern ignited in me a second ago goes cold. "She was suffering, Dad. She tried to ask for help, literally *screamed* for it—" I think of Margaret in the cemetery, when she saw the tomb. "And you wrote her off because you cared more about your own reputation than the wellness of a girl who might as well have been your own daughter."

It's harsh, but I don't care. He deserves every bit of it as far as I'm concerned.

"Don't tell me what I do and do not care about," my father says, his face growing red. "Clearly, you have no real concept of the position I'm currently in, with this estate, now that Penelope is gone. Those vultures are going to be looking for any weak spots to pick at, Lucy, and I refuse to show them any. We must persevere."

Of course, he's bringing up the country club yet *again*.

"What does any of that have to do with Margaret?" I say, challenging him on the issue at last. "It's not like those guys could actually have any significant impact on our lives. Just because the house has a history with a country club doesn't mean there are any legal ties. It's all about reputation. Margaret should have been more important."

"It's not as simple as that," my father insists, shaking his head angrily. "There are things that could be held against us. Circumstances…that give a few members of the club a certain amount of leverage with the estate. Serious leverage."

"Leverage?" I raise an eyebrow. How could a country club have leverage against us? "What do you mean? How much leverage, and what circumstances?"

I think about Gregory Shaw and Kent Dickens and all the other men who bring their wives for dinners and galas. If the leverage has to do with the estate, that must mean it's financial. But why would there be any financial ties between my family and the club? I have a sobering thought: *Is my father being blackmailed? For what?*

"It's nothing for you to worry about," he insists, looking remorseful for mentioning it in the first place. "Forget I said anything and trust that I'll take care of things."

Just like he took care of Margaret? I refuse to let it go. My mind spirals into questions and thoughts about the country club. Like why they don't play golf, or croquet, or any other sport like country clubs are supposed to. Actually, there are no organized activities at all, aside from the lush parties. I've also always found it kind of weird how they don't even have an official clubhouse—they always come here.

Everyone's always talking about the historical value

of this place. Whatever secrets are being held, whatever leverage that may be present…it must have something to do with the house itself.

"Back to the subject of Margaret," my father says in response to my silence, clearing his throat as he looks to his study at the end of the hall. "I never wanted to see her end up the way she did. I knew she was deeply upset about Penelope. I was able to see that when I discovered those photos. But her death wasn't something that could have been avoided *or* predicted, do you understand? Nobody could have seen this coming. Including you and me."

So that's it; that's as far as he's going to take it in his head. There are more important things to worry about, bigger fish to fry. I'm still reeling over his words regarding the club and the estate. Something isn't right there, I can feel it deep down.

"If this is who whatever you're hiding has turned you into," I say, "I think it's probably better that we give everything up and move away. Put this petty life out of its misery."

I see something now in my father's eyes that I've never seen before: fear. Fear at the idea of leaving our fortune behind, the lifestyle, the reputation tied to our name. Fear at the idea of having to provide for himself, something he's never had to do since he met my mom at boarding school. He was on a scholarship; she was not.

And now I think that it goes beyond my mother, and beyond his butterflies for the sister she didn't introduce him to until after they were already married. I think it goes all the way to the inside of his heart, where he needs to feel like he is important, like he matters in some way. It's his crutch, his appeal, the only thing he values about himself.

There is no chance he will ever leave the estate behind.

"This conversation is finished," he says and starts making his way down the hall to the study. "You've been through a lot and you need time, I get that. I think it's very important that you rest and take as long as you need to gather your head."

But I've already lost it, I think wildly.

There's no way we can live here just the two of us, practically strangers and hiding away from the world like rats in a place that was meant to be so much more than this nearly empty dollhouse made of stone. I wonder how long he'll be able to keep up the charade with nobody at his side, what he'll turn into after spending years living alone. If he thinks I'm sticking around for longer than what's legally required, he's insane.

Suddenly I remember something I was meaning to ask. "When are we having Margaret's funeral?"

My father stops closing the door to the study for a moment and clears his throat uncomfortably. "We're going to hold a memorial dinner in Margaret's honor next Saturday. Miranda is already hard at work with the preparations. There isn't going to be an actual funeral service."

The silence that follows his statement is cutting.

"What?" I say, not understanding. "What do you mean there isn't going to be a funeral?"

"Margaret has been cremated," my father answers simply. "Soon we'll have the urn and will be able to keep it in the parlor. Penelope would have wanted her to rest at home, not be buried somewhere far away after a generic service. We will honor her life at a memorial dinner with the club."

"Do me a favor," I say, raising a hand to stop him. "Stop pretending you're doing this as some sort of sentimental favor to Penelope, instead of wanting to hide what happened to Margaret."

Instead of answering me, my father closes the door to the study, and I am left, once again, in agonizing silence. No funeral for my cousin, all because my father sees her death as an embarrassing smudge on his precious reputation, another nagging complication in his plan to run the estate smoothly.

All my life I've been led to believe that the Acosta name was supposed to mean something special, but the older I get the more I realize how very projected that was; expectations by people with money who wanted to feel more important than they really were.

And those expectations should not have any influence over how we deal with life and death.

I ignore the urgent whispers in my head to go back to my bedroom and succumb to the glittery box of sharp edges and release, my only remaining friend... how disgusting. I don't have much to fight for anymore. I might as well give in.

I go up the stairs to the second floor, the stillness of the hallway smothering. After a few seconds of hesitation, I walk past my bedroom door, triumphant in my decision to say *screw you* to the idea of the box. If I really am a true Acosta, I won't lie down like a dog and give in just because things have gotten messy inside. I will outstubborn this, solve the puzzle, figure out what's happening to my family and why.

Maybe I have a chance, after all. With my heart in my throat, I open Margaret's bedroom door and step inside.

ELEVEN

THE LAYOUT OF the bedroom is identical to mine; mirrored from the wall we share. Margaret's room is infinitely messier, though—she hadn't cleaned in a long time, by the looks of things.

I look around, every familiar object radiating a different degree of pain: the indoor tent we used so many times in both of our rooms for sleepovers, rolled up around the poles and leaning against the corner of her dresser; the composition notebooks we often passed back and forth, taking turns with a story that we were imagining on the spot. Chocolate wrappers lie scattered around a coffee cup of colored pencils on the corner of her desk.

I wonder if she kept a journal, I think as I step toward the desk, my heart a hollow of hope at the idea of a single object that could tell me everything I need to know. I imagine pages filled with explanations, how she really felt about me, what she knew about Penelope.

The anticipation dies away as I dig through her desk to no avail, rapidly becoming desperation instead. I look in her nightstand, and underneath her pillow and mattress, and on the shelves surrounding her vanity, which is like mine but painted white. I look through the piles of notebooks for any I don't recognize. I look under her bed, which is mostly clogged with clothes and stuffed animals and crumpled-up drawings that Margaret apparently deemed unworthy but actually are pretty wonderful.

Once I've combed through the bedroom, I turn my attention to the closet, my final chance at finding anything. The white shutters on the closet doors are turned down, keeping everything inside hidden, and for some reason I am overcome with a wave of nervousness as I reach out to pull on the knob of the handle. The doors fold open in one swift movement, the wheels on the tracks squealing in strain. The only thing Margaret kept on hangers were her dresses for the club events, hung hastily in a row of lush fabrics in black and tones of jewel.

The floor beneath is littered with shoes, both sneakers and heels alike. I look on the shelf above the dresses, initially finding nothing except for spare blankets and old books from our childhood. But when I reach around the side of the blankets to see if anything's hidden inside, I discover that the shelf goes on farther than it appears to, an extended closet shelf that reaches inside the bedroom wall.

I drag Margaret's desk chair across the room and stand on it, moving the blankets out of the way to try to see if I can look down the hidden space. It's too dark to see anything, so I go back to the nightstand and grab a key chain I found while searching, a flat black disc that works like a flashlight when squeezed. Once back up on the chair, I can see the outline of something sitting on the shelf, closer to the end and out of reach.

It's got to be something, I think excitedly. *It's too out of the way to not be deliberately placed.* I use my hands to check the stability of the shelf, then cautiously lift myself up onto it. When I swing over the edge, my feet hit the old books and send them flying to the bedroom floor below. I lie still for a few seconds, on my belly, my hands and face pressed against the dusty shelf as I wait to see if the shelf will collapse or not.

It holds strong. I wince as I reach back to my skirt pocket for the key chain, still afraid of breaking the shelf and falling the seven-foot distance to the floor. I hold the little black disc ahead of me and press down with my thumb, lighting the way just a few inches at a time. I wriggle forward, sneezing twice as dust particles cloud the air around my face.

After I've moved forward a foot or so, I'm able to see that the object in the back of the shelf is a picnic basket, the top closed, the long arch of the handle nearly grazing the ceiling. I've never seen it before. I flip the top up but don't reach inside, afraid there might be spiders. After a moment I decide to tip the basket on its side so I can look straight in; when I do so, something rolls out before coming to a halt against my wrist.

It's a jar of teeth.

I gasp at the sight of them, all piled on top of each other with their roots all curved and yellow. There are at least twenty in the jar. My own teeth suddenly feel like they're squirming in my mouth. Why on earth would Margaret have hidden a jar of teeth in her closet? How did she even *get* these? Suddenly I'm bombarded by an old memory that I'd completely forgotten about until now, something that had to do with Margaret and Penelope, something that had to do with teeth.

Something that started in the attic.

I tip the light into the basket to check if there's anything else, eager to get out of the tiny enclosed space. Resting inside are a folded cloth, a few white candlesticks and a small bundle of what appear to be bones, bound with a string of brown leather.

I nudge the nightmarish jar back into the picnic basket with shaking hands, disgusted, then push it upright again. But something behind the basket prevents it from sitting flat, like it was before. I reach my hand behind the curved wicker corner and pull out a long wallet of shining black leather. I'm almost afraid to open it.

When I do, I instantly wish I hadn't.

It isn't anything like teeth or bones or clumps of hair inside the black leather wallet. It's a stash of alcoholic wipes, and a scalpel, and tissues dotted with old blood. I lie there with it unfolded in my hands, like some sort of messed-up doctor's kit, wanting to die. Margaret was hurting herself, just like I do.

And I'm the one who taught her how.

I'm overcome with a wave of dizziness. It's difficult to breathe up here; I need to get out, but all I can manage is to rest the side of my face against the shelf and try not to pass out. The attic. The teeth. Penelope. Margaret.

Scriiiitch. The sound is quiet, a little muffled and coming from right next to my head. *Scritch, scritch, scriiiiitch…*

It sounds like fingernails being raked across the inside of the wall.

That's just rats, I tell myself in my vertigo. *Put the wallet back and get the hell out of here, now.*

I scramble to fold the awful black wallet back up, then slide it behind the picnic basket against the back wall. *You've lost your mind as much as Margaret did,* my mind screams at me as the scratches against the inside of the wall become more frenzied, desperate, *angry.* I'm reminded instantly of the scratches on the wall in the attic, when Margaret made me cover my eyes.

I knew then that I used to be afraid of the attic, but I couldn't remember why. It wasn't the boxes of my mother's things that scared me away. It was something else.

"Lucy," I suddenly hear, a pleading, muffled voice coming from in the wall. "You won't believe how much it hurts to be dead."

I let out a strangled moan, in disbelief at what I'm hearing. *No,* I think wildly, remembering Margaret tearing up as she told me about hearing the voice of Penelope. *No.*

"Be quiet," I say out loud without even meaning to, my voice frail. I scoot backward out of the tiny, terrible space, flinging myself down as soon as I possibly can, missing the chair completely and falling to the floor.

Once I'm up again, I don't bother to put back the blankets I took down from the shelf, or the books that I accidentally kicked. I leave Margaret's room without taking a single thing, no photos, no art, no reminders of a life that was once here and now isn't. I somehow manage not to run.

There was a voice in the closet. And now all I want to do is cut myself into shreds.

I can't let myself be driven to madness, like Margaret was.

Once back in my own room, I lock the door, take the glittery cigar box from my vanity shelf and open it to remove the purple flick lighter from inside. Then I close the box and walk across my room, shoving it into the ashes of the fireplace. I arrange sticks around and over it like a little house, then use the lighter to set the sticks on fire.

I watch until it's gone, turned into molten bubbles of melted glitter and glue, smothering the glowing red-hot tools inside. *It's done now. No more.* When I'm satisfied it's been destroyed, I take off my clothes and climb into bed, rubbing my fingers over the lumps of scarring that web the skin of my hips and thighs and knees.

No more counting, I promise myself, only allowing the tears to come once the covers are over my head and everything is black. *No more counting scars or you are going to lose your mind, if you haven't already.*

But I'm sure that I already have. For the first time since I found the jar of teeth in Margaret's closet, I recall the memory of what happened all those years ago in the attic.

TWELVE

WHEN I WAS ten years old, I hid in the attic while playing hide-and-seek with Margaret. The mostly unused room rested above the back end of the third floor, musty and dark and crowded with boxes that were filled with my dead mother's belongings. For that reason, I knew, it would be the last place Margaret expected me to hide. For once, the joke would be on her.

It doesn't bother me in the slightest, I told myself as I found a flashlight and crawled around the rows of stacked cardboard boxes. I hardly remembered my mother at all. Why should it be scary for me to be near her things?

I made my way to the corner of the room, the one farthest away from the closed door on the attic floor. The flashlight illuminated the hardwood floor that reached ahead of me like a hallway between two walls of boxes. *Eva*, they all said on them, written in my father's hurried hand.

I suddenly wondered if I was doing this to prove something to Margaret, or to prove something to myself. I brought myself into a crouch behind some of the boxes, not wanting to go any deeper into the attic. If I could manage to stay without getting too freaked, I'd break Margaret's hiding record for sure.

I contemplated turning off the flashlight but decided in the end that I could leave it on until I heard my cousin coming. I pointed it toward the floor for good measure and was surprised to see that the thick layer of dust ahead was disturbed, as if someone had been there before me. I shone the light back to where I'd come from to confirm my own footsteps in the dust, then ahead again, to the area where I'd not yet tread.

Someone had been in the attic recently. Strange.

My curiosity got the best of me, and I lifted the beam to lighten the area beyond where I crouched, an open circular space made from all the *Eva* boxes. In the middle of the circle were a few things, but it was too hard to tell what they were without getting closer. I stood and stepped into the enclosed area, my breath held in my chest, my eyes wide at the sight of the items on the floor—a single candle, a sheet of paper and a knife with a short, curved blade. The paper looked like it'd been torn from a journal and burned around the edges. And on the wood beneath the knife, there was a cluster of dark droplets soaked into the wood.

Blood.

My heart in my throat, I got down on my knees and picked up the leaf-pressed paper, realizing almost immediately that it was a poem. It was written in my aunt Penelope's handwriting, a mix of print and cursive that scribbled over the page in two short, jagged stanzas of black ink:

The Mother sings a hungry song
of blood and cracking teeth.
She dances in the dark below,
wants to pull us underneath.

Her claws, they rise, they sway in dance
to the melody of screams.
Her lullaby will never end,
till the world comes apart at the seams.

As soon as I finished reading it, I dropped the poem back onto the floor with a little gasp and scrambled to make my way out of the room as quickly as I could. Screw sitting around in the dark alone after reading something like that. Why was that even up there? And where did the blood come from?

I wanted to tell Margaret, but finding the right way was impossible. I felt like no matter how I did it, my cousin would only freak out and find a way to turn it into one more thing to hold against her mom. What I had found in the attic scared me, but I still felt protective over Penelope. To imagine her upset or embarrassed because of me was awful.

So I held it in, at least for a week. I thought about it every time I talked to my aunt and started searching her face for any type of clue that might explain why she'd be sitting in the attic with a bloody knife writing poetry about that terrifying "Mother."

An Acosta must always mind her own business. The amount of times I had to repeat it to myself over the following days was beginning to become overwhelming. I'd sit in my room alone, gazing at my pretty box of razors, itching to grab it and bring it to the space between my bed and the wall, use the blades to let all that dread pour out of my body.

No, I would scold myself. *Stop being weak. Save it for things that actually matter. Have some control over yourself, loser.*

Soon I stopped fearing whatever it was that I'd found in the attic and started being more afraid of my impulses. When I'd first started, it was easy to control when I chose to do it; that was part of its supreme satisfaction, the important and liberating moment where I took it upon myself to carefully use drastic measures to create that perfect balance.

Now that urge was creeping up on me, uninvited, strong, *insistent*.

Later, Margaret interrupted my train of thought when she came into my bedroom without knocking, something that was always a pet peeve of mine.

"What?" I nearly yelled, causing her to raise an eyebrow over my irritation.

"I need to talk to you about something," she snapped right back, crossing her arms over her ribs. "Or are you too busy sitting in silence and doing *nothing* at the moment?"

I sat up and straightened my shirt, folding my hands over my lap. "Sorry," I mumbled. "I was just thinking about something, is all."

"My mom?" she asked seriously, which caught my attention enough to make me forget all about the box of razors. How did she know?

"What about her?" I asked, struggling to keep my composure. *I will not tell her about the attic!* I swore to myself again.

"I could have sworn you were acting weird around her lately," Margaret said, pulling my chair with the green velvet cushion across the rug to rest in front of me. She sat in it and crossed one leg over the other. "Why is that?"

It's a test was my first reaction, which brought a little relief. *She doesn't know anything, so she's trying to trick you into saying something...*

"Nope," I said with a straight face, not blinking. "What are you talking about?"

She studied me for a moment before accepting my answer. "This is a weird thing to say," she said, clearing her throat and picking a thread from the knee of her leggings. "But, um…"

I waited for her to continue, my expression frozen.

"I'm pretty sure my mother is some sort of witch," Margaret finally said.

Despite everything, I couldn't help but laugh. "A witch?" I said. "I'm sorry—did you see her fly around the courtyard on a broom or something?"

Then I remembered the candle and knife in the attic, and my smile faded.

"I walked in on her doing…something." Margaret shifted her weight in her seat, keeping her eyes anywhere but on mine. "She had set up some sort of, I don't know, ritual-type area."

"Ritual?" I asked. I tried to imagine my aunt chanting nonsense words, wearing a black pointed hat, but it just didn't gel.

"There were bones," Margaret said. "And…teeth."

The Mother sings a hungry song, of blood and cracking teeth…

"Stop," I said, my heartbeat quickening at the memory of the poem. "So what would that even mean, then? If she really thought she was a witch?"

"You believe me?" Margaret asked, as if in disbelief.

"I thought you'd be telling me to get lost if I told you about this, but I had to at least try. It's been..." She paused, bringing her hand up to her mouth for a moment. "It's been really bothering me, Lucy."

Suddenly I felt terrible about how certain *I'd* been that I could never tell Margaret what I found while playing hide-and-seek. I never would have told her, yet Margaret was able to tell me. She always was the better friend.

"I saw something in the attic," I admitted, and her eyebrows flicked up. "I think that's probably why I know you're telling the truth."

"I knew you were lying!" She kicked my foot and crossed her arms, but her expression showed relief. "So what are we going to do about it? Like you said before, what does this even mean?"

I strained my mind for reasons why Penelope would do witchcraft. Did she think it really worked? She must have if she'd gone through enough measures to get *teeth*. Human or animal? I didn't want to know.

"I'm not sure," I said honestly. "I guess the only thing we can do is keep a close eye on her. It's not like she'd ever hurt us." In a chaotic mess of confusion, I knew this one thing to be true.

Margaret sighed but nodded. "Okay." Her eyes darted away, and I realized there was still something bothering her.

"Hey, Marg..." I said gently, and her mouth pulled

into a pained frown. "What was she doing with the teeth?"

My cousin didn't answer for a moment. She took a deep breath and stood, turning her back to me to head for the door.

"She was swallowing them."

THIRTEEN

THE WEEK PASSES by in a blur of long naps and frantic research sessions regarding ways to get away from this house as quickly as possible.

I discover that there is such a thing as year-round boarding schools and start making a list of potentials to consider, purposefully seeking out any that are geared toward teens with psychological or behavioral problems. Something tells me that I would fit in at a place like that. Maybe I'd even benefit from it. And if not, well, at least I won't be here. The grounds of the estate are enormous, but after everything that's happened, there are only a few places that I can even stand to be.

I'm too scared that I'll hear a voice in the walls again, like in Margaret's closet. Nothing has happened since then, but I know what I heard. *Lucy,* the voice said, so pained, so desperate. *You won't believe how much it hurts to be dead.* I only considered telling my father about it for a brief second before remembering how he reacted when I told him that Margaret was hearing voices.

And what about Penelope? Is it possible that she was somehow a real witch? At the time I had convinced myself that my aunt was secretly a tortured artist of some kind, and that the poem about the Mother was just some sort of expression. And the teeth... I had never let myself fully believe Margaret. I refused to think about it for more than a second, forced it out of my mind until it disappeared. Maybe she sensed that somehow. Maybe that had something to do with how she treated both Penelope and me.

I can no longer handle going into the garden, or the courtyard, or the entry room, where Margaret's brass urn sits centered on the mantel. I don't return to Penelope's room. I stay away from Margaret's. I pretend that the third floor doesn't exist at all. The library is all right as long as I avoid looking out the window toward the forest, but even then, the only place at this point that can offer any sort of comfort is my bedroom.

On the day of Margaret's memorial dinner, I wake to the sound of rain falling hard against the window. I wonder what would happen if I didn't show up tonight, or maybe claimed that I was sick, which is true in one way or another. Deep down, though, I know I have to go—my cousin didn't even get a funeral, a fact that still doesn't sit right with me. This dinner will be my only chance to show my respects.

When evening is approaching, I go to the kitchen for a cup of tea when I run into Vanessa, who I haven't seen since the night Margaret died. I was certain she'd quit, but here she is rolling dough out over the floured island counter. Penelope's recipe book sits propped open within view.

Vanessa looks up when I enter the kitchen, but she goes back to what she was doing as if I'm not here. Relief. I head for the cupboard with the tea, then fill the kettle and set it on the stove to wait. As it warms up, I look over Vanessa without shame, since she's standing with her back to me. The last time I saw this girl, she told me that my cousin and I seemed fucked up.

And that was *before* Margaret jumped out the window and I started to hear things. I'm trying desperately to believe that what I heard in that closet had to have been similar to what sometimes happens when you're sleeping at night and wake up to see a shadowy figure in your bedroom, or a tarantula lowering from the ceiling. You're awake, but your mind doesn't care; it shows the thing to you, anyway, trickery of the mind, a waking nightmare. That doesn't mean it's really there, though.

Instead of my mind playing tricks on my eyes, it's playing tricks on my ears, that's all. I'd believe it with the amount of emotional stress I'm under.

"I'm..." Vanessa looks up from the dough for a moment, breaking the silence. "I'm...really sorry about what happened with Margaret. I couldn't even imagine—"

"No," I say, cutting her off. "You couldn't." Why bring it up in the first place? Vanessa only knew Margaret at her worst, so it feels phony and ridiculous for her to show even a small amount of pity when it's clearly forced. I might as well start getting used to it, though, with the memorial dinner happening tonight. I'm sure they'll all act like they loved her to pieces.

"I may not know what it's like," she says softly. "But I'm still sorry that it happened."

"Thanks, I guess."

She goes back to her food prep and I suddenly feel bad for being so cold. It's not her fault that I'm cracking up. Still, though, it's for the best. If she knew about half the shit that was toiling away in my brain, she'd be running for the door.

"I keep going over that night in my head," she continues, and I wish so much that she'd shut up. "I still can't believe that it happened."

"Look," I say. "I know she wasn't the nicest or anything. Especially considering the rat on Miranda's pillow, but you have to understand—"

"I'm sure it didn't help the situation at all, though, me getting all confrontational like that." She pauses. "I'm just...sorry."

I don't want to think about what could have been,

or what should have been; it doesn't do anything but make things worse. I turn the heat on the stove up to high, very much wishing that the stupid water would boil.

"It's fine," I say in a quiet voice. "I'm sure it would have ended the same way regardless."

She takes the hint and stops talking after that. Soon the kettle begins to whistle and I can't fill my mug quickly enough. "Later," I say as I walk past her to the door, only because it feels too weird to not say anything. She doesn't reply.

I drink my tea and then read in bed, opening the window just an inch so I can fill my lungs with long, deep breaths of the sweetly fragrant rain-kissed air. This has always been my favorite kind of weather. With a belly warm from tea, I roll onto my side and close my eyes, trying hard not to think about Margaret and how on a day like this we would have been painting our nails and watching old musicals in her room or mine, maybe even asking Penelope if she wouldn't mind baking some fresh brownies or something. How things change.

I've destroyed my box in the fireplace, but I'm always still aware of the shining black leather wallet tucked up in that secret hiding place on the top shelf of Margaret's closet. I should have taken it and thrown it into the fire, too, I know, and now I'm too afraid to go back and get it. Not because I'm afraid I'll use it, but because I don't want to hear that voice again, all shoved into that cramped, dark space. If I can help it, I'd like to stay away from that room forever.

I don't know if I can take something like that again. I know deep down that I'm broken in some way, a way that needs help from someone else to fix, or at least to get to a better place. But the weight of the situation makes admitting everything to my father feel impossible. I won't be able to explain everything without breaking down at least once, and that would be the point that he stopped listening to send me away with disgust on his face. Maybe if I showed him my scars, he would listen, but the idea of doing that makes jumping out the window seem a whole lot easier.

If only Margaret was here.

The hole of grief inside me throbs; the pain of it nearly taking my breath away. The sound of the raindrops against the glass changes, morphs into something that sounds a lot less like water pattering over a window and a lot more like nails scratching over wood. I keep my eyes closed, focusing on the sound that should go away but doesn't.

Scritch. Scritch. Scriiiiiitch—

"Lucy," Margaret's voice echoes through the wall, very slowly, as if she's in immense pain. "Help."

I open my eyes, gasping as I sit up quick enough to make myself dizzy. The sound of fingernails on drywall stops. My heart thuds in my chest.

The room is empty. "Margaret?" I say, not caring how silly it'd look to someone else. Her voice sounded so real, so close. But, of course, there's nobody here. I am alone.

I didn't think I was sleeping.

Even with the door closed, I can hear the commotion from downstairs as Miranda and Vanessa move the furniture in the parlor around to prepare it for the guests. I should probably get ready for the memorial dinner. Maybe it'll help me let Margaret go a little, stop letting this stress affect me so much. *What if it's not stress?* my mind whispers, and my heart leaps at the thought. *What if it's a ghost brought here by witchcraft?*

What if it really is Margaret?

I get ready quickly and put on the same black dress that I wore at the last club dinner. It's much more appropriate for this occasion, anyway. As I descend the grand staircase into the entry room, I notice right off the bat that there are fewer guests than last time, which makes me feel insulted on Margaret's behalf.

I can see through the dining room door that the table is almost set up for dinner, which is a relief. The less talking and condolences I have to withstand, the better. I nearly jump a foot when I notice that someone has placed a blown-up, framed portrait of Margaret next to the urn on the mantel—I was not prepared to see her face.

I see Gregory Shaw and Kent Dickens standing over

the food table, talking to one another with serious expressions. Their wives, Nancy and Mary-Anne, stand closer to the bar, chatting with another group of members who appear to be talking about the pros and cons of various lawn treatments. How mournful.

No sign of my father yet.

I see Vanessa come in to gather empty plates from the table, and she catches me looking at her just before Nancy Shaw hurries over to lead me back to the group, gripping my clammy hand in her satin-gloved one. Her lips are just as brightly painted as last time, but a different color.

"Oh, Lucy, honey," she says, giving my hand a little squeeze. "We were all so devastated when we heard about Margaret, the poor little thing. You two were always so close. And on top of Penelope missing, my goodness, I just can't believe it."

Don't forget Walter, I want to say, feeling a little mad, but I know they've forgotten his name by now, so I don't bother.

"Thanks, Nancy," I say and squeeze back limply, trying to smile but failing. "I can't believe it, either."

The group stops talking about the lawn treatments as soon as we step up, and starts regarding me with solemn nods and *I'm sorry*s instead. People take turns telling endearing stories about Margaret, every single one of them from when she was too little to talk much, fancy that. Even in death, people can't find things about my cousin that they liked

"Poor Penelope," says a man named Duncan, whom Margaret and I always referred to as The Monopoly Guy. As kids, we never remembered his name, only the likeness he shared with the silly board game mascot, so even after we found out his name, we still called him by the nickname. "I'm almost glad she's missing if it means she didn't have to endure the pain of losing a child."

I stare at him, not caring if my expression is murderous.

"I'm not," I say, recognizing the same edge that my father's voice sometimes gets when he's becoming angry. "Glad that Penelope's missing, I mean. And you shouldn't be, either."

"Of course not," the man's wife cuts in, nudging him slightly with her elbow. "I don't think he meant it like that, my dear."

The Monopoly Guy's face reddens. "Of course I didn't mean it how it sounded, dear child. Forgive me."

Miranda steps into the entry room and announces that dinner is being served. I notice that she looks much more run-down than usual, frazzled even. Her previously warm smile has been replaced with a stressed grimace as she motions people in. I imagine how crazy her job must be and feel gross inside, guilty, even though she's here of her own free will.

We make our way into the dining room, which is lit by dozens of candles that sit, weeping, in the gold holders mounted all around the walls. The tables are loaded with all of Margaret's favorites, paella and cheeseburgers and blueberry pancakes with turkey sausage and fried eggs. I can't help but smile at the array; there is something weirdly satisfying about seeing a silver platter piled high with an elaborate pyramid of cheeseburgers. Margaret would have loved this, said that it reminded her of something from Hogwarts.

She also would have loved the looks on the guests' faces as they take in the dinner options, like they've never seen any type of food that wasn't caviar or a whole roasted pig. "Breakfast for dinner," Gregory Shaw remarks from a few seats down, with a little too much enthusiasm. "Now, that's something I can get behind."

I hope you choke on it, I think as my father enters the room from the kitchen. He stands at the head of the table and taps his glass of pink lemonade—another Margaret favorite—with a spoon.

"Thank you all for coming tonight," he says, looking up and down the rows of faces before him. "The shock of Margaret's passing is something that has blindsided the family, of course. We're just devastated to have these losses pile up so quickly like this."

I see Gregory Shaw shoot Kent Dickens a look, his brow raised. I wish I knew what he was implying,

and I'm suddenly wondering what they were talking
about so seriously before dinner was called. Plans on
horning in on the estate now that the family is weak-
ened, maybe?

My father clears his throat and is silent for a moment.
I notice for the first time that his hair isn't combed to
the side as usual, and lies in soft waves over the top of
his head. I remember how Miranda appeared similarly
drained. This situation is sucking the life out of us all,
even if for different reasons.

"We're filled with a great sadness," my father continues, his eyes lowered, his voice strained. "But I think
it's safe to say that after tonight her soul will have been
sent off properly. Most of you have known the girls
since they were babies. It means so much to us that
you'd come tonight to show your support."

Yes, I'm so sure that Margaret would have been just
thrilled to know that even The Monopoly Guy showed
up for a free five-star meal at the Acosta estate. I wonder for the first time how many details these people
know about my cousin's death.

"To Margaret Anne Acosta," my father says, lifting
his glass into the air. "May she rest in peace."

"To Margaret," we all say in unison, our glasses
raised. I take a short, uncomfortable sip, all too aware
that most of the eyes in the room are on me.

Clinking glasses and sipping pink lemonade in her
honor doesn't feel right when I know what she went

through in her final days. The cemetery, the attic, the claims she was being haunted. I should do something about it, I decide. If I try to ignore what's happening, I might end up just like Margaret. The voices have started already, after all.

People begin to serve themselves once the toast is finished, chattering quietly about frivolous things, which I much prefer over ignorant comments about Margaret or Penelope. It seems that nobody's quite sure how to handle the array of choices; the people who grab cheeseburgers stay away from the paella, only filling the rest of their plates with things like french fries and corn on the cob, leaving the breakfast dishes untouched, as well. I take a little of everything, which is clearly the point of the dinner, although I'm not exactly starving.

How am I supposed to be satisfied with this as closure for Margaret, especially after my father hinted at some sort of leverage that the other club members could hold against him? I scan the crowd, desperate for any sort of clue, but everyone is too focused on their food. My father doesn't eat at all, just stares alternately between his untouched plate and the watch around his wrist.

Whatever it is, they're spreading him very thin. Could it really be blackmail? A situation where someone in my family pulled something illegal in order to obtain or hold the estate? It'd have to be something of that scale; why else would it be such a threat? Did Penelope know what was going on?

Once the dinner platters are taken away and replaced by trays of desserts, people start mingling in the parlor again, taking their nightcaps from the bar before offering their condolences to me or my father again and heading out. I need to use the restroom but don't want to go all the way upstairs, so I make my way down the hall toward the one by the study instead.

I'm almost to the end of the hall when I hear voices coming from inside my father's study. I stand close to the door and peek in, hiding from view when I see that Gregory Shaw and Kent Dickens are standing next to the desk with drinks in their hands.

"Look at this place," Kent slurs, clearly drunk. "What does Felix even *do* in here? He doesn't work on anything hard enough to need such an extensive office."

"I'm guessing Penelope used it far more than he did," Gregory says and takes a gulp of his wine. "God only knows what she ever saw in that idiot."

I bite my lip but keep silent. *Jealous bastard.* I remember what my father had said about Gregory being rejected by Penelope.

Kent bursts into a sloppy laugh. "They probably had sex all over this desk."

If Margaret was here with me, she would kill him herself.

"Have some respect," Gregory says, unamused. "That woman was the shining jewel of the Acosta family. Nobody expected that everything would be left to Eva. She never had much interest in upholding the tradition of the estate. It was such a joy when Penelope was able to take over."

I nearly cry out in response. The only reason Penelope was able to *take over* at all was because my mother *died*. How dare he?

"Am I the only one who feels like all of this is a little fishy?" Kent looks through a folder of papers that is open on the desk. "First Penelope goes, and now her daughter? Did Felix even say how she died?"

"No," Gregory says, his voice grim. "Only that she became suddenly and severely ill."

I knew it. My father wants to hide what happened to Margaret, do whatever it takes to keep the club's opinion of our family as high as possible. If he wasn't capable of taking care of a teenager, how could he manage an entire estate? Nobody would ever know how plagued my cousin was with pain, how much more complicated she was than they'll ever give her credit for.

"Yes, well," Kent says. "She seemed perfectly fine the last time we came for dinner here. How convenient that the only remaining Acostas are Felix and his daughter. Maybe they're—"

That's it.

"Get out of here," I say, stepping into the study, my blood buzzing. Kent jumps and gapes at me, Gregory narrows his eyes into a cold stare. "How dare you come into our home and talk about my aunt and father like you did just now? Both of you are assholes."

"So sorry, Lucy," Kent says, red-faced and scrambling to get out from behind the desk. "We were just taking in the house, wandered a little too far, I admit—"

"Oh, a little too far, is that all, Kent?" I nearly spit. "Get the hell out of here. *Now.*"

He rushes by me and leaves without Gregory, who is still standing with his drink in hand as he takes the sight of me in.

"Excuse my rudeness," I say, unblinking. "But I believe I asked you to get out."

"So sorry about Margaret," Gregory says, walking slowly around the back of the desk. "She was an extraordinary girl, indeed."

"Leave." I step aside, leaving the doorway nice and open, but still he lingers in the study.

"I know you and your father weren't too keen on what I said about the estate last time I was here," Gregory says, taking a leisurely step forward. "But Margaret seemed to click with it, didn't she?"

I think about starry-eyed Margaret at the last club dinner, and how she stuck up for Gregory after everybody had left. But that was because of how she felt about my father, I know. The grudge had nothing to do with Gregory.

"Let's get something straight," I say. "You don't know anything real about Margaret, or why she felt how she did about the estate. You probably didn't even know Penelope that well, as much as you may have wanted to."

His composure falters for a moment. He tries to cover it by taking another swig of his wine.

"You're a pathetic, insecure old man," I continue, still enraged that he would try to use Margaret against me. "Make no mistake. My cousin *hated* you." It's not the entire truth, but I don't care. "Now get the hell out of my father's study before I cause a *real* scene."

Gregory Shaw's glare sharpens—he stares at me like I'm an insect that needs to be crushed. I suddenly wonder if he's one of the club members with leverage over the estate. I wouldn't be surprised at all. *Let him try to intimidate me*, I think. *I'm not scared of him at all.* What's he going to do, hit me with a stack of cash?

Gregory sets his glass down on my father's desk, then makes his way to the doorway. When he passes me, he pauses for just a moment to look down into my eyes.

"I'm going to hold back on saying anything too harsh because you're in mourning," he says, his voice lost of the usual pretentious charm. "But I will say this. The women in your family have been dropping like flies lately. If I were you, I'd watch myself."

"Is that a threat?" I ask, but he's already heading down the hall. "Gregory, are you threatening me?"

He's gone, and I am left in a quiet study that still stinks of their obnoxiously potent cologne. When I'm sure the hallway is empty and nobody can see me, I take Gregory Shaw's glass of wine and throw it against the wall, shattering it.

FOURTEEN

THE NEXT MORNING at breakfast my father asks about the broken wineglass in his study. I tell him that I saw Gregory Shaw and Kent Dickens loitering around in the hallway and that Gregory had been drinking wine.

"That man is a detriment to the club," he says angrily and sets his newspaper down on the table. "One bad apple *will* spoil the bunch here. I'm sure by now that he's turned most of the other members against me. They won't back me down. I can prove myself to them."

"Why would you even want to?" I ask, hoping to get a little more information about what kind of pull certain club members may have. After my encounter with Gregory last night, I can't imagine a thing in the world that would make me want to prove anything

to him. If he had the power to get us out of the estate
and take it himself, why wouldn't he have done it by
now? "What about this place is so worth fighting for?"

My father sets his coffee cup down, hard enough
to cause the dark liquid inside to slosh over the edge.
"We live in a historical landmark tied to the club and
a name that is worth being proud of," he snaps. "Do
you think I took the act of changing my name lightly
when I married your mother? That I just did it for the
money, and not for Eva and what she wanted to con-
tribute to this club? Because if so, then you're just like
them."

"But she didn't even want this life," I burst, remembering what I heard last night. "It was Penelope that
did."

Let him know that I know. The secrets are too much
to stay hidden by now, too relevant. They could even
be dangerous.

"Who told you that?" my father asks, squinting as if
I've said something profoundly stupid. "Your mother
most certainly *did* take her reputation seriously. It
wasn't as glowing as Penelope's, I'll admit. They had
two very different ways of looking at the potential of
this place, but to say that she didn't want this life...
She wanted it all for you!"

My face flushes hot. "It's something I heard Gregory
say," I admit. "Something is going on around here and
I think that he might know what. I think you might

know, too." At the very least, he's hiding information about whatever leverage the club has over our family.

Aside from that, there's another thing that doesn't add up to me—why everyone always talks about the *potential* of this place, as if it's something more important than a place being used for parties. And they're not even a real country club! At this point, only an idiot would try to pretend this is all normal. Yet, even now, my father still won't admit the truth to himself: we should be running.

"Enough," he finally says. "This is your legacy, Lucy. Embrace it and you'll be set for life, as will your children, and theirs."

"I have no interest in living here any second longer than I have to," I say. "It's boring, it's empty and, apparently, it's corrupt."

It's not just the club I'm thinking about now: I'm also thinking of the scratching sounds in my room, like fingernails scraping across the walls. And I'm thinking about the moment I found the jar of old, gnarled teeth, and about Penelope believing she was a witch. I'm thinking about Margaret's voice in the darkness of the closet. I can't imagine a single piece of information that would convince me it was all worth it.

"It's *more* than that," he insists, leaning back into his chair with a sigh. I notice he didn't correct me on my use of the word *corrupt*.

He rubs his fingers over his temples as though he

has a headache. "This sort of opportunity, this lifestyle, never would have been possible for me if I hadn't met and fallen in love with Eva. It's a once-in-a-lifetime opportunity to live like a king. If you want to play on this level, upholding the tradition of the estate with a club that doesn't ask for much in return, you've got to sharpen your teeth."

"For what?" I cry out, unable to speak calmly any longer. "To protect a *legacy* of being a party host? That's all you are to them!"

"There are plenty of people who would love to take our place," he snaps, hitting his hand on the table, causing me to jump. "I don't know about you, but I don't plan on letting them anytime soon."

"Honestly, I wish you would." I nod angrily as I stir what remains of my oatmeal. "That's not honorable, Dad, that's just sad."

"You never would have said any of this to Penelope," he scolds, disgust evident in his tone. "You respected her more than anybody else, and yet you criticize me for doing the exact same thing she was? For upholding the life that she valued?"

I can't explain to him why it's different now, why I'm not so sure anymore that I ever knew my aunt in the first place. The teeth, Margaret hearing her voice, the blood splatters on the attic floor I found when I was a kid. All of these are things he would refuse to listen to. All of these are things that would have him send me to a hospital of some kind.

Maybe that wouldn't be the worst thing in the world. There's nobody for you here anymore.

"I don't care if you understand or not." My father stands, leaving the paper at the table instead of bringing it with him like he usually does. "I'm going to continue running the estate, no matter how many people are against me. I will overcome this for her."

I wonder if he's talking about my mother or Penelope.

"I'll never understand what you're fighting for," I call after him. "I'll never understand *you*." I want him to hurt like I do now, feel the weight of my disrespect over the entire situation.

"I'm sorry to hear that," he says, not sounding very sorry at all. Again, I become angry at myself for feeling hurt. He finishes leaving the room, and I breathe in slowly through my nose to keep from breaking another glass. At this point, I feel like I'm just sitting around, waiting to die.

I rise to bring my dishes to the kitchen, wondering what I could possibly do to fill another day before I can go to sleep again. Browsing faraway schools has become a habit, but I think it may be eating away at me from the inside, all those quiet hours surrounded by nice things and swirling wallpaper. I remember again how I thought I heard Margaret say my name in my bedroom before the memorial dinner last night.

I wonder if things will get even worse; how could they not?

Nobody's in the kitchen, which is a relief. I sigh and load the dishes into the dishwasher, and as I'm leaving I can swear I hear the sound of someone crying. *Not again*, I think. *This is not happening again.*

It sounds like it's coming from outside, in the courtyard. With a deep breath, I open the glass door of the kitchen and step out. Vanessa sits with her back against the wall, crying into her hands. She doesn't notice me until I'm standing over her.

"Hey," I say after a moment, wrapping my arms around myself in the cold. "Are you okay?"

"No." She wipes tears from her face with both hands. "No, I am not."

I've never been able to stand the sight of somebody else crying. It's too vulnerable for me, not okay to plague other people with, but then again, nowadays I wish more than anything that when Margaret had been crying in her room at night, I had gone over to see if she was okay. Plus, Vanessa could be crying because she saw or heard something disturbing. If she did, I need to know about it.

I sit beside her on the ground.

"You've got enough shit going on," Vanessa says. She doesn't seem irritated that I sat down by her. "You don't need to listen to mine, too."

"I can't really disagree," I admit with a humorless

chuckle. "But I think I'll try, anyway. Did something happen?"

Vanessa's eyes well up again. *What is it?* I want to cry out and grab her by the shoulders. I remember how terrible Miranda looked at the memorial dinner. "Is it about your mom?"

"Yeah," she says, struggling to keep her voice level. "How did you know? It's like she's starting to let the stress of planning these stupid events get to her so badly," she says, then stops as if she's said something wrong. "Sorry."

"Don't be," I say. "They are stupid. *Really* stupid."

So she isn't out here crying because she heard or saw something crazy. I guess I should have known, it really could be my head making all that stuff up. But now we've gotten too far into the conversation to end it quickly without being rude.

"Well, they're definitely not worth losing sleep for," Vanessa says. "She never does anything for herself anymore. It's like she lives to serve this place, to serve *Felix*." She says his name with a touch of resentment. I don't blame her for it, not one bit.

"I'm sorry if he's been demanding lately," I say awkwardly, feeling somehow responsible. "He takes this stuff way too seriously, and with everything else that's been happening—"

"It's not that," Vanessa says. "Not exactly. I mean, he has been kind of demanding, but I think my mother might have some sort of silly crush on him. It's obvious to me that the feelings are not reciprocated, but she's totally unreasonable about it."

Miranda is setting herself up for supreme disappointment if she thinks there is any chance that my father would ever return her feelings. He's so obsessed with Penelope, there isn't room for anything else in his head or his heart.

"She wants to be able to take care of *everything* Penelope would have done," Vanessa continues. "So that he can rest and take it easy and mourn. These last two dinner parties have taken so much out of her, and now she's already on to planning that holiday party, of course..."

I forgot all about the winter holiday party. It's always been a major, grand event, the biggest of the year. I refrain from telling Vanessa that the planning for it will likely be about four times as intense as the planning for the smaller dinner parties.

"Miranda should take a vacation," I say, wishing they'd just go. Let him see what it's like to live *like a king* without anyone willing to serve him. "After everything that's happened since she started here, she deserves a break." I pause. "I think what she probably deserves most is to quit."

"I tried to convince her of that, actually." Vanessa sighs in frustration. "She keeps saying that everything here will crumble without her, but I really think she's just running away from everything back home. The divorce was starting to get really ugly when she applied to live here. I'm pretty sure she'd do anything to get away from it all. That, and she wants to impress Felix."

We stay quiet for a few moments, looking out over the courtyard that is riddled with dead rosebushes. When the cold season ends, the roses will bloom again, just in time for galas and brunches and cocktail hours for the club that will apparently continue coming here forever. *There may be a pretty bow tied on top of it all*, I think bitterly, my eyes wandering the length of the courtyard. *But to me, it's still hell.*

"Look," Vanessa says, her voice soft. "I'm sorry to load all of this onto you. This is the last thing you need right now, to hear someone complain about your father and all this stuff that's out of your control."

But my whole life has been out of my control, I would tell her if I wanted to tell the truth. *No matter how much I wanted to pretend otherwise.*

"No," I say, looking her in the eye. "I'm glad you told me. Keeping stuff like that inside can lead to some pretty horrible things."

I think of the secrets Margaret kept from me: the picnic basket, the contents of the shiny black wallet, whatever else she knew but never told.

"Yeah," she agrees, then starts to stand from where she sits against the wall of the house. She brushes dirt off the back of her pants as I stand, too. "Thanks for listening. And, Lucy... I'm also sorry about what I said to you the night Margaret died. About you guys being fucked up."

The comment had bothered me at first, but compared to everything else that happened that night, it's practically irrelevant by now.

"Don't worry about it," I say, suddenly light-headed at the sight of the forest in the distance. "You weren't wrong."

"Well, maybe I wasn't," Vanessa agrees. "But it's not like the same couldn't be said about anybody, really. We all have bad stuff."

"Mmm-hmm." I make my way to the door, anxious to get past this strange conversation with the cook's daughter. We may all have bad stuff, but I'm starting to think that what's wrong with me may be irreversible, especially since hearing the voice in the closet. Maybe that's the way it was with Margaret. Maybe our paths are one and the same.

No, I tell myself. *You burned that box for a reason. You will not kill yourself like Margaret did.*

"Anyway," Vanessa says, holding the door open for me. "Sorry about that. I think I just needed to get it all out. I know that I, for one, feel like I'm losing it sometimes."

"You're not alone." I head inside, where Miranda is prepping the ingredients for lunch. She stares at Vanessa and me with unblinking eyes. "Hi, Miranda."

"Hello, Miss Lucy," Miranda says, shifting her focus to the knife she's using to chop an onion. She doesn't look up again. "I hope you're doing okay."

"Hanging in there," I say, feeling awkward about what Vanessa just told me about Miranda having a hopeless crush on my father. What could she possibly see in him besides money? "I just wanted to tell you that Margaret's dinner last night was very nice. Thank you for doing it in a way that she would have loved."

It's not exactly the truth, but the reason last night was horrible had nothing to do with the food, so in a way it isn't a lie, either.

"Of course, honey." Miranda looks so surprised at my words, it makes me feel even worse. "It was no problem at all. I only wish I could have done more for Miss Margaret." She looks down again, her eyes glazed and red. "Vanessa, would you mind starting a soup pot with some olive oil over medium-high?"

"Of course, Mama," Vanessa says, going for the cupboards right away. "It was...nice talking to you, Lucy."

She's a bad liar, but I won't hold it against her. It wasn't nice for me, either.

"Okay," I answer instead of saying *you, too.* She grins weakly and raises a hand to wave. "See you around."

Upstairs, my bedroom is cool and dark, since I never opened my blinds after getting up this morning. I'm standing in the middle of it, looking around quietly as I try to figure out a way to investigate Penelope's supposed witchcraft further. Maybe there was something missing in her room, I didn't exactly comb it over before because I was only wanting to look at the photographs that Margaret ruined. There could be something else in there. Evidence, maybe.

I sit on my bed with a straight back in silence, my hands in my lap, staring at the gold swirls on the wallpaper and wondering if I could possibly gather the courage to go check out that cemetery in the forest again. But no matter how I look at it, I can't figure out why it'd be a good idea to visit somewhere that could have potentially had to do with what happened to Penelope and Margaret.

Don't forget Walter, I remind myself. *It's almost like his death is what set everything into motion.*

I can't believe this. I'm actually sitting here entertaining the fact that my aunt was messing around in something real. But…what if? Things can only be so coincidental.

The thing is, if I'm willing to believe the witchcraft is real, what does that say about Penelope? What were her intentions if she was really swallowing teeth? Was it a ritual of some kind? A curse? Was there someone she was trying to hurt, or was there something she was trying to protect? She was so dedicated to the estate, maybe the ritual had something to do with protecting it.

Thinking about all of it makes my head hurt. There's

no way to know what my aunt's motivations were, no matter how well I thought I knew her. I rub my hand over my shoulder, trying to loosen some of the tension that is causing my head to ache. I really don't feel well.

"It hurts," someone groans from behind me, where the wall is. I jump from my bed with a shriek, turning around only to see that nothing's there.

It's happening again. I no longer believe my mind is playing tricks on me, because this can't be fake, not unless I've cracked and spilled my mind like oatmeal onto the floor.

There come more sounds, this time too quiet to hear from where I stand. I move closer, slowly, my hands clasped onto each other as I force myself to breathe. The house makes a great settling sound, and I move the side of my face against the wall to hear the voice inside, rambling in an urgent tone.

"My head is wet," it says quickly, barely audible through the wall. "It's wet and sticky and who's in there with you? Who's in there in that room with you right now, Lucy?"

I jerk my face to look behind my shoulder, my spine electric at the thought of someone standing behind me. But there is nobody. The shutters on my closet are open. My mouth slacks open as I move my ear back against the wall.

"What did you find in my closet?" the voice demands

in the same quick urgency. "Were you snooping in my closet, Lucy? What did you find in there?"

The voice belongs to Margaret.

FIFTEEN

"MARGARET?" I GASP, my eyes wet. I lean away from the wall, trembling. My body feels hollow, no insides, no muscles, no bones. My head swims, and for a moment I think I'm going to pass out. "Is this real?"

"Please don't leave me," her voice says louder than before, clear enough to understand but still muffled by the wall. She speaks as though she's stuck in endless panic. "You have to be here for me now. You were never there for me and you have to *stay*, Lucy..."

So this is it. Either I've lost my mind or I'm about to find out firsthand exactly what the hell is going on with this estate. Either way, hearing Margaret's voice means, unquestioningly, that I will be dead soon.

I start to cry.

"Best friends," she murmurs sorrowfully. "We were best friends."

The fear is electric, making my blood hum, making me rock back and forth.

"We were," I say with a cracked voice, terrified, hardly aware of what I'm saying. "We were best friends."

"Until we weren't anymore," her voice continues, so frantic, so at unrest. "I don't understand it, Lucy. Why didn't you *believe* me? Why did you just *let me die…?*"

I put my hand against the cold wallpaper. Margaret, it's my Margaret, *I miss her, I love her, she's dead.* I think about how after I found Walter, I couldn't stop thinking about how I was going to die. I could never have imagined anything that started like this, hearing someone dead speaking to me from inside the walls.

My scars itch beneath my clothes. "I didn't mean to," I cry, pressing my face against the wall. "I tried to figure out what was happening with you. I'm so sorry about everything, please…"

"My head," she nearly weeps, loud enough for me to startle and take my ear away from the wall. "It hurts, Lucy, it hurts so bad…"

My pulse intensifies, and I raise my hand to cover my mouth. I think about the grotesquely loud sound her head made when the iron spike of the garden fence came through the back of it, the pieces exploding out into the grass, scalp, skull, brains. I think about the sick gurgle that came from whatever was left.

"Are you trapped here against your will?" I ask,

upset all over again about the fact that I couldn't catch her in time before she jumped out that window. "Why is this happening?"

There comes a pause, followed by several little clicks on the wood. I remember with a shiver how these very sounds had come from behind me in the attic when I was covering my eyes with my hands. *It wasn't Margaret doing it.*

My cousin's whimpers are cut off by a guttural sound from deep inside the wall that reminds me, overwhelmingly, of the song of cicada insects in the summertime: a shimmering veil of clicks made from the vibrating of frail membranes on thickened ribs, softened by the bedroom wall.

When it fades away moments later, I don't hear anything else. My head is light.

"Margaret? Margaret!" I step back to the wall and put my hands on it, my cheek, my forehead, begging her to come back while I cry all over the wallpaper.

We were best friends, she said to me. *Until we weren't anymore. Why did you just let me die?*

Have I gone mad?

No, I try to insist, but can't deny the confusion. *Think about everything else that's happened. This is real, it's happening and now you're all caught up in the web and you'll never get free.* I sit in the silence for an hour, the dread and anticipation building with every breath, but nothing else happens. I finally manage to stand up, my legs and back sore from sitting on the carpet.

Something is causing Margaret's soul to be trapped in the walls of the house. She was telling the truth about hearing Penelope. Is there a way to help? Or is this just a dead-end spiral to an early grave?

I shudder as I think back on my cousin's final days. So many signs leading up to what happened, and yet all I could manage to do was sit around and worry about it. If it's even a little bit my fault that her soul is...in whatever state it is, I have to help her if I can. If I don't, I'll never be able to live with myself.

I scour my mind for anything that could help me piece this together. No matter how many ways I look at it, the conclusion is always the same: the start of Margaret's demise was my aunt's disappearance. Is it possible that Penelope did this? Gregory Shaw? My father?

If so, how is the house involved? Is Penelope's soul still trapped in the walls like Margaret's? Does the history the country club has with the estate play a role in this...haunting, if that's what it is? Who can I trust, if anyone?

The situation is so overwhelming that it makes it nearly impossible to do anything except sit in a twitchy, paranoid heap near the wall where I heard my cousin's voice, hoping every moment that she'll come back and tell me something that will help me figure out what's going on and how I can help her. I think about my box, dead and melted in the fireplace, and the wallet in Margaret's closet, very much alive.

After the sun has gone down, there is a knock on my door.

"Who is it?" I call without standing up.

"It's me," Vanessa's voice answers from the other side of the door. "You're not in bed yet, are you?"

I stand up, cringing as I realize that my legs are asleep. I go to the door and open it to find Vanessa standing there. "I didn't see you eating dinner with your father, and then you never came down to get something afterward. Just wanted to make sure you weren't hungry or anything."

Suddenly I remember how withdrawn Margaret was before she went off the deep end. She skipped meals, acted reclusive. I can't let myself fall into that same pattern if I want a chance at breaking this cycle. "I could eat," I answer, forcing myself to sound as normal as possible. "I guess I lost track of time."

I'm not sure what I thought waiting around would accomplish, especially after so many hours of silence. The memory of talking to Margaret feels so far away, like it was in a different world. I need to force myself to be proactive through the fog of confusion and fear.

"Are you all right?" Vanessa asks as we walk down the hall toward the stairs. "You don't look so well. Did something happen since we talked this morning?"

Like hell I'm even going to try to explain any of this

to Vanessa. There is no way she'd be able to offer any sort of support or belief.

"Not really," I say. "I just think the weight of everything is finally starting to catch up with me. I might be overly exhausted."

"I hope my complaining earlier didn't have anything to do with it." Vanessa trails behind me slightly as we go down the stairs. "Although, how could it not?"

"It's fine," I assure her. "Seriously. It was nice to think about something else for a while."

"Yeah, I get that," she says. We head through the empty dining room and into the kitchen, which smells richly of garlic and tomato.

"You missed spaghetti night," Vanessa says with phony enthusiasm, taking a plate from the oven and setting it on the counter. "And we even made meatballs."

"Thanks for keeping a plate for me." I look at the plate, piled high with noodles and sauce and a big hunk of garlic bread. "That looks really good."

"It's fine." Vanessa shrugs, then heads to the fridge, where she pulls out a bowl of salad. "I set this aside, too."

"Great," I say, grabbing my food and taking it back with me to the dining room. Vanessa follows, sitting across from me at the table. Before hearing Margaret's voice, I would have wanted her to stay away, but now I can't help but admit that being around someone else feels nice, safe. While I eat, she looks around the room with her arms crossed over her chest.

"It must be so weird to eat all of your meals in an epic dining hall," she says as I dip my bread into the sauce. "This place is almost like a castle."

"Kind of," I say, taking a moment to give the place a quick look-over. "I guess I don't really notice the size of it anymore. I wish I could live somewhere smaller, cozier."

Somewhere that isn't haunted.

"That's what I like," Vanessa says. "Cozy is good. Warm, comforting, safe."

"Where's your mom?" I ask, trying to change the subject.

"In bed already," Vanessa answers. "Although, I wouldn't be surprised if she's working on the lists for the holiday party while she's lying down. She just will *not* give it a rest. I try not to worry, but it's hard."

"I'd worry, too," I say, nearly delirious in my exhaustion. "Things around here aren't right, and she looked so tired the last time I saw her. It's almost like—"

I pause, realizing what I'm about to say. "Actually, never mind."

"No, what?" Vanessa wants to know. "You have to say it now! You've passed the point of no return."

It's proving to be harder to keep this all in than I thought it would be.

"I was just going to say that it reminded me of how

Margaret looked a few weeks before…you know." I raise my hands quickly when Vanessa's eyes widen "But then I realized that it was a totally inappropriate comparison. Something…*happened* to Margaret." I remember waking up to find my cousin standing over me with the pair of scissors. "Miranda's just strung out."

Vanessa relaxes a little bit, but I could swear her posture is just a little more rigid than before. I regret planting the idea in her head, awakening whatever paranoia was lingering dormant in her worry. If only she knew what sorts of things were really happening in this house.

After I'm done eating and my plates are in the dishwasher, I try to engage in more small talk with Vanessa, but it's too hard to focus on anything besides Margaret and Penelope, trapped in the walls. Will I be able to hear my aunt's voice eventually, too? Is anyone else's soul trapped?

If I won't go out to the cemetery, maybe I should take a look around the attic. There may be something hidden in one of the boxes that have been up there since before I found the knife and the creepy poem. The more I think about it, the more nervous I am at the idea: Who's to say there isn't a ghost waiting for me up there, ready to push me out the window or worse? Then again, if I haven't run screaming to my father to be sent away by this point, I must not care that much about what happens to me. At least not more than I do about finding out exactly what's happening here.

To avoid letting Vanessa think it's something personal against her, I fake a headache and get upstairs as quickly as possible, lingering at the top of the second floor until I know she's gone. My stomach heavy, I make my way up to the third floor in the darkness of the parlor.

When I reach the top, I pause. It's hard not to go over what happened the last time I was in this hallway, stumbling between my father and Vanessa as they led me away from the attic, hysterical. Panic rises within and I find myself unable to go to the miniature staircase that ascends into the ceiling of the back corner of the house.

You need to be strong, I scold myself. *You need to do this for Margaret.* The silence of the third floor presses in from all sides as I struggle to slow my breathing. After a few minutes of standing there in trembles, I feel my foot slide backward toward the stairs. I take a step back, then another, then turn around and go quickly down to the second floor.

Within minutes I'm sitting on my bed against the wall, resting my head on it, determined to stay awake in case Margaret comes back. While waiting, I fall into a deep sleep, still sitting upright against the wall. I'm awakened when there comes a crash from downstairs, loud enough to make me jump. Then, the sound of footsteps rushing back and forth across the tile flooring, multiple sets of footstops. A shout

I'm too startled to move. I sit with my knees pulled to my chest, listening as the commotion dies down and eventually goes away completely. *What is happening?* I think wildly as I hear the sound of more footsteps, this time rushing down the hallway outside my door. *Is this reality, or hell?* For a moment I imagine Gregory Shaw breaking into the house to murder everyone inside.

My doorknob rattles as somebody tries to open the door. When it's discovered that the door is locked, there comes a quick, fierce series of knocks. "Lucy," someone says. I make my way over to open it, my heart racing, my hand over my chest.

Vanessa is standing in the hall, her eyes wide, her mouth hanging open.

"What's the matter?" I ask. "What happened?"

"It's your aunt, Lucy," Vanessa says, her voice shaking. "She's back. Penelope's alive."

SIXTEEN

THE WORLD STOPS TURNING.

"What?" I say, breathless, sure that I misheard Vanessa. "What did you say?"

"She walked into the house without turning on any lights and accidentally knocked something over in the dining room," Vanessa says. "My mom and your dad are tending to her now. She was so freaked out, like she didn't understand where she was. I had to tell you."

For the first time since I heard the voice in the darkness of Margaret's closet, I feel like it's possible that everything might somehow turn out all right, after all. Penelope is back and I know she'll tell me everything, especially if I'm straightforward about knowing about the teeth and the poem and the blood on the attic floor.

I finally manage to speak. "Did she say anything about where she'd been? Why she came back?"

Vanessa looks down to her feet, shaking her head back and forth. "To be honest, Lucy," she says, her tone low, "I don't even think *she* knows where she was."

I stare at her, my mind a whirlpool.

"She wasn't injured," Vanessa says, "but something was...wrong. She was filthy, from her hair to her clothes to her smell. And I've never met her before, but I'm assuming she wasn't usually as disconnected before she disappeared."

"Disconnected?" I ask. I can feel my pulse in my ears. *But she's back.* "What do you mean?"

"She wasn't answering Felix's questions. She seemed terribly confused," Vanessa says, her expression troubled. "She would ask weird questions about Margaret but then act like she had no idea who that was a moment later."

Does that mean she had something to do with what happened to Margaret? If so, can she free my cousin's soul?

"But where did she come from?" I say, hardly able to believe it. "You said she was in the dining room?"

"We think she came through the kitchen, from outside," Vanessa says. "There were dirty tracks on the floor, and pine needles all over her feet."

Pine needles. I remember the sight of Margaret running in from the forest not ten minutes before she ended up dead. She'd told me that she had gone to see the cemetery in the woods. Just the thought of the place turns my stomach. Has Penelope been wandering the woods this entire time? How did she survive?

"I have to see her," I say, motioning for Vanessa to step out of the doorway so I can go.

"I don't think your dad will let you," Vanessa says with a regretful tone. "He made a point to tell me not to tell you, to let you rest and that he would fill you in when morning came, but—" she shrugs at me "—I thought you'd want to know now. I knew you would, actually."

"He won't find out that you told me," I say, gently pushing my way past her. "I'll just say that I heard the racket downstairs and ask what it was."

"Okay," Vanessa says, clearly relieved. "Thank you."

We walk toward the main staircase in the dark, not speaking at first. I feel electrified, buzzed, like I drank an entire pot of strong coffee. If Penelope's back, that means she wasn't dead, like everyone imagined. A chilling thought goes through my mind—who had Margaret been talking to, then?

"I'll see you tomorrow," Vanessa whispers when we're in the entryway and about to go our separate ways. "I don't know whether to be happy about this for you or what. It's just so weird."

I know what you mean, I think. "Thanks for telling me about my aunt."

"Of course."

The house is completely silent, which is unsettling in a way that counteracts the adrenaline rush I was experiencing a moment ago. The crystal chandelier in the parlor looms overhead, a glittery ghost in the dark. I walk through the shadowy room, stepping over a toppled houseplant, the grains from the soil sticking to my bare feet as I make my way across the tile. When I step into the hallway behind the parlor, there is light streaming out from underneath Penelope's bedroom door. I make my way down the hall, heart pounding, but before I can reach the door, it opens and my father steps out.

"Hi," I say, and he nearly jumps out of his skin.

"What are you doing down here?" he asks in a hushed voice. "Please go back upstairs."

"What was that sound I heard a few minutes ago?" I say, feigning ignorance. "It freaked me out."

"I don't have time to explain this to you right now," he insists, his voice a harsh whisper. "I promise I'll fill you in tomorrow morning, but for now I have to make some arrangements and I'm afraid it absolutely cannot wait."

Doctors for my aunt; I can tell by his urgency. Despite the worry in his brow, he seems so much lighter than before; he's clearly relieved by Penelope's return. It will mean a lot for the club, and for him. I wonder if he swallows teeth, too.

"I…" My mind races for a way to force more information. "I could have sworn I heard Penelope's voice, and now her bedroom light is on."

The silence is tense. Finally, my father sighs in frustration. "Yes," he says, "but she needs medical attention and I don't want to overwhelm her. I need you to please go back to your room and wait until morning. This is a wonderful thing, Lucy. She's back. She's *alive.*"

No matter how many times I hear it, I still can't believe it.

"Is she all right?" I ask, my voice breaking a bit. "I just want to know what's going on. Please let me see her, please?"

He stares at me for a moment. "Seeing you may set her off again," he says slowly. "She's very confused and gets spooked easily. We finally got her to rest in bed. Miranda's in with her now. Just give her a few hours to breathe."

My stomach drops.

"This is why I didn't want to discuss this right now," my father says upon seeing my face. "I don't want you to be upset, Lucy. You should be happy." He reaches forward and puts his hand on my shoulder. I don't remember the last time that we hugged. "We've just gone through the worst month of our entire lives and now we've been given a gift. It's so important to be aware, grateful even."

He acts as though nothing permanent has happened.

"Grateful?" I ask, bewildered. "How do you think Penelope is going to feel when she finally realizes that Margaret is dead?"

"One step at a time," my father insists, growing impatient. "And tonight is not the night for you to see her."

She has to have answers for me about Margaret somehow. There's no way she won't know *something* that can help, even if just in the slightest.

"Fine," I say, accepting defeat. Just her presence is making things seem less dire—there's hope now, lots of it, a light at the end of this tunnel of utter madness. "I'll go back upstairs and wait to see her until tomorrow. Let her rest."

"It really is best," my father says and heads back toward his study to make whatever arrangements he's planning. "Thank you for understanding."

I pretend to leave, but when I hear the door of his study close behind him from around the corner, I creep back into the hallway, to the door with the light shining out from underneath.

"Rest," I hear Miranda say in a low, soothing voice. "Everything's okay now, I promise."

"How long has it been?" Penelope's voice says, weak and uncertain. "How did I get back here after all that time?"

"It's been nearly a month," Miranda answers. "Do you know where you've been?"

"I've been home," my aunt croaks. "Haven't I? I was at home all this time, with my new mother…"

I bite my lip as I listen. New mother? Penelope's mother is dead; she has to mean the Mother from the poem I found in the attic years ago. But what is she? Who? I don't remember the poem verbatim, but I do remember being terrified by it, something about a melody of screams and blood and cracking teeth.

Teeth.

Sometimes, people do rituals for gods that they want to honor. Maybe this Mother is Penelope's god.

"No," Miranda says. "You haven't been at home, not for a long time, and Felix has been worried out of his mind. But that's okay now, everything is—"

"Something went wrong," my aunt interrupts. "It wasn't supposed to turn out like this."

I think about Margaret's voice from inside the walls, so tortured, so desperate. It's all my fault that she's there. I was so sickly selfish, too tangled in my own webs to help her get through hers, or even just *listen*, for God's sake. I have to find a way to free her. If I die trying, at least we'll be together again. I almost can't take this anymore.

An angry thought flashes through my mind: *it's not just me to blame.* There's a reason her soul is trapped in the walls in the first place, and Penelope has to know something about it.

There comes a creak from beside me and I realize

my father is about to open the door to his study. He must be done making his phone call already. I sprint down the hall and barely make it around the corner before I hear the door open, followed by the scuffle of slippers on tile.

I rush back upstairs, adrenaline pumping once again. I pace my room with fervor, trying hard to make sense of what I heard just moments ago. Clearly, something happened to my aunt to cause her to be so clouded and strange. Does this mean she won't be able to answer my questions about what's going on? Is she really the one who started all of this? *Something is wrong*, she said. *It wasn't supposed to turn out like this.* If she's been doing rituals...

What if that's why she disappeared—she was doing a ritual? My mouth slacks open at the thought. A ritual in the forest? At that cemetery, maybe? Margaret and I didn't see anything when we went out there except for gravestones and the tomb, but I can't deny the significance of the place—Margaret did visit it an hour before her death and spoke of it like it was somewhere special. It has to be relevant.

My mind goes wild with theories on how Penelope's ritual could have gone wrong—she could have messed it up, or someone could have interfered. *Or*, I think with just as much dread, *the ritual could have gone right, and she just didn't know what she was doing. Or maybe she did.*

Do I even know my aunt at *all*? Did I ever?

I promised myself that I would stay here to help Margaret. If I call the police, who knows what they'll unveil with the country club? It could end with my father in jail and me being taken away somewhere, and then my cousin would be stuck in hell forever.

Suddenly I can't stand the sight of my bedroom for another second. The wallpaper, the eerie tension of feeling like I'm being watched, the fireplace where my box still sits in a ruined pile of ash and rummage. I flee from my room, going straight for the bathroom down the hall. I lock the door behind me and crawl into the claw-foot bathtub that's surrounded by a thick scarlet curtain with gold embroidery. I pull the curtain closed and sit back in the cradle of shining white porcelain, struggling not to scream.

Stop it, I think as my body starts physically reacting to the panic, my lips trembling and my breath heaving and my eyes open without seeing. *Stop it, stop it, stop it.* As I sit there shivering, my eyes fall upon the dainty metal basket that hangs over the side of the tub, filled with soaps and salts and…a razor.

I lean forward and snatch it so roughly that a handful of greasy bath oil beads scatters all over the bottom of the tub, gathering around my legs and feet and making the air smell like peaches. Just feeling my fingers wrapped around the tacky pink handle is comforting; these types of razors can't do too much damage, anyway, especially if I'm careful…

"Fuck it," I say aloud, finally accepting that I can't do anything more about it.

I lower the blade to hover over my wrist when a muffled voice cries out from somewhere behind the tiled wall.

"Please don't," it wails, and I recognize the voice immediately as Margaret's. "Don't do that, Lucy. Don't do that anymore. There's been too much blood already, too much blood and too much death..."

I drop the razor and grab the sides of the tub until my knuckles are white, as if I'm spiraling out of reality and need some sort of anchor in the storm. After the electrifying moment passes, I weakly roll to the side of the tub and lean my head against the wall, the checkered tile cool on my clammy cheek.

"Margaret," I say, beginning to cry. "I'm so sorry, about everything, *everything*..."

"You have to fix it," she pleads, and I hear the sound of her fingernails scratching frantically against the inside of the wall. "If you don't, my head will never stop hurting!"

"Tell me how," I burst. "Tell me what to do."

There's a strange pause then, a silence that draws on long enough for me to wonder if she's gone. I'm about to take my ear away from the black-and-white tile when I hear it.

"Your mother, Eva, is in here, too, you know," Margaret says, her tone low and even. Her words make my heart skip a beat, make me stop crying immediately, make my breath catch in my chest. "And she isn't very happy with you."

"That's not true, sweetie," another voice chimes in, terribly equal amounts of familiar and unfamiliar, and my hand flies to cover my mouth. "I just miss you so very much and it's taking you too long."

My mother is trapped in the walls, too, and even more tears come. I wish I could say that her voice brings me comfort, fills that massive gap that exploded into existence once Penelope and Margaret were gone, but all I can feel is despair, more so now that I realize she may have been watching me grow up, seeing who it is that I've turned out to be, what I've ended up doing to myself. Some daughter, even to a ghost.

"Too long to what?" I manage to ask.

"To either save us or join us," my mother says. There come a series of insect-like clicks and hisses from behind the tile all of a sudden, the sounds of gasps and splintering bone. *"Join us."*

Without trying to speak to them anymore, I lean away from the wall and put the razor back into the basket, then stand, nearly jumping out of my skin when I step on a waxy bath oil bead that explodes with a sharp pop. Without cleaning the mess up, I open the scarlet shower curtain and step out, my stomach in my throat, terrified that any second some invisible force is going to slam me against the bathroom tiles and peel my skin off strip by strip or something worse.

But nothing happens, nothing stops me from leaving the bathroom, and no more voices await me in my bedroom. Regardless, I pull my bed away from the wall and leave it, exposed, in the center of the room. Sitting straight up, I stare into my fireplace, unblinking, my arms wrapped around myself as I wonder about things like madness and murder and just what can possibly come from swallowing a bunch of teeth.

SEVENTEEN

I END UP skipping out on sleep altogether, which may not be the greatest choice, but then again, it isn't much of a choice at all. Every time I come close, I'll hear some sort of sound—a winded tree branch scraping against the glass, a popping ember from the fireplace, the sighs of the house settling—and be certain that it was Margaret or my mother.

I can't decide if they want to protect me or hurt me. Margaret stopped me from using the razor on myself, but my mother begged for me to join them. How else would I join them without dying? I remember how Margaret mentioned that there was some sort of way to free her. I'm doing all of this for her. She deserves for me to either figure it out or die trying.

Maybe I'll end up joining them, after all.

By the time my father comes to get his food for

breakfast, I'm already dressed and waiting at the dining room table.

"I'm ready to see Penelope," I say as soon as he walks into the dining room, despite the grim expression on his face. "She's had the night to rest."

"Fine." My father's hair is not combed sideways with gel; he is not wearing a suit. "You can try to see her whenever you want, and the nurse can be the one to tell you if it is or isn't a good time."

"There's a nurse here?" I ask, thrown off. "From the hospital in town?"

"Privately funded," my father says. Of course. "Penelope didn't want to go to the hospital. She keeps saying she only wants to stay home, and after what she's been through, I don't blame her."

"Something's happened to her." I stand from the table and suddenly realize that I'm still wearing yesterday's clothes. "She's not the same."

"She will be." My father pours his coffee and turns to lean against the table. "She'll come back to us as she readjusts, little by little, and then maybe she'll let us know what exactly she's been through, and how she survived all this time."

"I wonder what Gregory Shaw and Kent Dickens will think," I say, hoping to gauge some sort of reaction from him. "Do you think they'll be happy or sad?"

My father stiffens. "I'm starting to become worried about you. You don't look well at all. I'm starting to wonder if Margaret's death has had an especially ill effect on you. Perhaps some extended rest will—"

"I don't need to rest," I snap as I walk past him, out of the dining room and into the parlor. "I need to speak with my aunt."

Once at her door, I knock hesitantly, unsure if I'm ready for whatever is about to happen. Will Penelope be happy to see me, or will it make her upset? Will she help me stop the living nightmare, or will she drag me deeper into it? What will she say when I tell her I know about the teeth and the rituals and the Mother? What will she say when I ask her if she's purposefully trapped the souls of Margaret and my mother in the walls?

Before I can wonder any more, a tall man in a brown houndstooth suit answers the door. In his hand is a syringe.

"Yes?" he says, as though he has no idea who I might be. Surely my father mentioned that he had a daughter who lived here.

"I'm here to see my aunt," I say. "I'm Lucy."

"Oh, Lucy," the man says, looking thoughtful as he steps to the side to let me in. "Your name has come up quite a few times in Ms. Acosta's ramblings, so it's a pleasure to finally make your acquaintance. My name is Howard."

"You don't look like a nurse." I eye the empty syringe still clutched in his hand. "Aren't you supposed to be wearing scrubs or gloves or something? And what's that for?"

"I just had to sedate her," Howard says, dropping the syringe into a plastic biohazard container, ignoring my other comments. I step inside and look to my aunt's bed, almost hesitantly. Sure enough, there she is, lying against the pillows, her mouth slightly open as she sleeps. I wonder why she needed to be sedated.

I don't know what I expected, maybe some obscene display of evil or insanity or God knows what else, but seeing her now for the first time in weeks only makes me think of old times, when she was so loving and protective of me, like I was a second daughter. No matter what it is she's been caught up in, there's no way she would ever really hurt me.

The question now is if she hurt other people, like Walter, and Margaret, and my mother.

"Penelope," I whisper, and her eyes stay closed. I rush to her side before I even know what I'm doing, sitting at the bedside chair and taking her hand in mine. *I don't have to take much more of this; she's here and it's all going to be over now...* "You're really back."

My mouth pulls into a hard frown as I take in my aunt's appearance close-up. Her hair is filthy, saturated in oil and dirt, and the tangles look like they'll take days to get through. Besides that, it's also thinned noticeably, and there are strange sores scattered randomly over her skin. Her lips are spiderwebbed with cracks.

"Is she sick?" I ask.

"A little," Howard says, his deep voice calm and smooth. "The lacerations were probably made herself, with her fingernails or something from outside. The cuts just got a little infected, is all. The fever will stay down eventually, with my help. She was also suffering from extreme exhaustion—it's as though she hadn't slept for days. It made her extremely paranoid. The sedation will help with that immensely. After she's had a solid sleep, she'll be much more like herself."

I look at Penelope's face, willing her to open her eyes and tell me everything, but she remains still.

"Has she been outside all this time?" I think of the forest, and the cold weather, and all the rain we've been having. "How did she survive?"

"I don't understand it," Howard says, sitting in a different chair and staring at Penelope with a wary eye. "She's clearly been through *something*, but it's not consistent with someone who's been unsheltered this entire time. There's no hypothermia or any other of the more severe symptoms of extended cold exposure, but she wasn't wearing any shoes when she came back in. The bottoms of her feet were affected by walking bare over the terrain of the forest, but just barely."

Penelope's hand is hot and clammy in mine. I imagine her barefoot in the forest, saying nonsense chant words and dancing through the trees in the midnight snow, and my chest becomes heavy with dread.

"It's almost as if she was confined somewhere," the nurse in the houndstooth suit continues. "Perhaps she was staying in an abandoned mine or cave or something of the like."

I think of the white marble tomb in the woods, so stark among the trees, and my heart skips a beat. Did the ritual require her to somehow get inside the *tomb*? I imagine Penelope lying silently inside when I ran my hands over the marble, looking for an inscription when Margaret and I found the cemetery, and my hands start to tingle.

But as I get up and pull my hand from Penelope's, her eyes flicker open and she looks up at me. "You," she says, her words thick and slow from the sedation. "My niece."

"That's right." I sit back down immediately, leaning close. I take her hand again, smiling softly while I look into her eyes, telling myself over and over not to be scared of her. "Hey there, Penelope, welcome back. I missed you more than you could ever know."

"She should be sleeping," Howard says from behind me. I hear him fumbling with something in his bag—likely more sedation drugs. I have to hurry.

"I'm not there anymore," Penelope rasps, taking in a ragged breath of air. "In the darkness."

I stiffen in my seat.

"Nothing to be alarmed about," Howard says when he sees my reaction. "The medicine I gave her is strong.

She just needs a slightly increased dose so we can at least get eight hours of sleep into her. Talking nonsense is completely normal."

"What darkness?" I ask my aunt as he preps the injection, ignoring his words. "Why were you in the darkness, Penelope?" I want to ask specifics about the ritual stuff but can't in front of whoever this Howard person is. I don't know who he is, but if he's privately funded, he could be connected to the country club somehow, and therefore cannot be trusted.

"Best not to indulge that sort of behavior," he says, sounding confused. "Just keep talking to her as though she never said it. Reassure her that she's fine."

"She's not fine," I snap at the nurse, who looks at me like I've grown a second head. I turn back to my aunt, who is gaping up at me with wide, terrified eyes.

"I did something bad," she whispers. "I'm so sorry."

"It's okay," I say back, even though I'm pretty sure it's not okay. "There has to be a way to turn it all around, right?"

The nurse raises an eyebrow, and I wish more than anything that he would go away.

"Maybe," she moans, her eyes desperate. Her speech is running together; the sedation drugs are pulling her back into sleep without even having to receive the second dose. The nurse nods to himself, content, and replaces the cap on the injection needle.

My aunt lowers her voice to a whisper—I lean in

close so that Howard won't hear. "It's because the grounds are so sacred," she says. "It never could have happened otherwise."

From the time that I was little, Penelope would refer to the estate as sacred. Clearly, she meant it literally. But how did it become that way? Was it always that way, or was something done to make it sacred? Suddenly I'm overcome with the urge to discover everything I can about the origins of the estate itself, from before it was in my family.

"Rest now," I assure her, which Howard must approve of, because he finally sits back in his chair. She won't be able to help me while she's this drugged, and at least now I've finally got something productive I can do in all of this. "We can talk when you're a little more awake."

A tiny glimmer of hope shimmers cruelly away inside. My aunt is asleep before I've finished rising from my chair.

"I'll come back later," I say, and Howard nods. "Please make sure I'm told when she's awake again, and not so drugged up."

"Of course," he assures me. "We'll get her there, eventually."

Hopefully by then I'll know more about what is happening in this house.

I leave my aunt's bedroom and head up the stairs to the second floor, passing the bedrooms and curving around to the other side of the house, where the library is. I haven't been in here since I promised myself I'd stop staring out the window, wishing for Penelope to come back. And I thought things were bad then.

The floor-to-ceiling windows that make up the back wall of the library are covered by enormous curtains, filling the room with shadows. I make my way to them, intending to open them wide so I can see what I'm doing, but then I notice the dull glow of a reading light in the corner of the room. I make my way over, passing the shelves until I see who is sitting in the dark, reading: Vanessa.

At first my mind goes wild, trying to find ways to get her out of here—she can't know what I'm doing! But then I realize, if I'm able to talk her into helping me look around for stuff on the estate, I'll maybe be able to find what I'm looking for twice as fast, two brains and all that. At this point, I need all the help I can get. And it wouldn't be endangering her, right? Pulling her into a bigger picture that she's not even aware exists? It's only simple research about the house, I decide in the end.

She'll be fine.

EIGHTEEN

"HEY," VANESSA SAYS when she sees me, hiding her startle well. "Sorry, I've just never seen anyone else in here, and it's been a nice place to come in between stuff with my mom. There's so much cool stuff on these shelves, it's crazy."

I think of the time I found Vanessa crying in the courtyard, about how working here had taken its toll on her and her mom. She even said that she thought Miranda had a crush on my father, which makes me wonder how Miranda's been reacting to Penelope's return. I can imagine why Vanessa would want to get away from it all in the library—I know from experience how great of a hiding place it is.

"Yeah," I say lamely. "Thanks for telling me about Penelope, by the way."

"Were you able to see her last night?" she asks. "That whole thing was so damn weird."

"Not last night, but this morning," I say. "And the circumstances aren't exactly favorable, but I'd much rather her be with us than dead." *At least there's hope now.* "Anyway, thanks again. I appreciate it."

She shrugs, then looks back down to her book. "Were you wanting to sit here, or...?"

"No," I say, suddenly feeling uncomfortable just standing there. I head over to the curtains and open them wide, filling the library with sunlight. "I'm just trying to find out some stuff for a history project I'm doing."

"Oh," she says distantly, still reading. "Cool."

I wander over to the nonfiction shelves, too embarrassed to flat out ask for help. Instead, I remember the time Penelope called me into her room to make sure I was okay after I'd found Walter, how there'd been stacks of leather-bound books all over the floor. I peer through the books in front of me, most of them with bright, commercially printed covers.

"What's the project for?" Vanessa asks, looking up from her own book. "History can be fun."

"It's about this house, actually," I say as casually as I can. "I have to do research, but I've put it off for too long and now I'm stressing."

She nods, and I spot a cluster of books toward the end of the shelf, all leather-bound, one of them with a small red page marker sticking out the top. My heart leaps at the sight of it.

"Maybe I can help somehow," she says and closes her book. "I'm bored out of my skull."

"If you want." I head toward the book with the red page marker. "How good are you with search engines?"

"Are you kidding?" she calls, and I can hear the smile in her voice. "I'm an expert, just like everyone else."

"Maybe you could look up some stuff for me while I check out these books," I call back. The spine of the book is bound in black leather, and the words *A Guide To Post-Mortem Examination* are stamped down the side in gray ink. My pulse intensifies as I stare at the title.

I hear Vanessa get up and head across the other side of the room, where the computer desk is.

"What are we looking for, exactly?" she calls over once she's sat down.

"I was hoping to find any information I could on the origin of the estate," I answer. "Before it was in my family. I need to find out everything I can about the original owner, or anything about the land, if possible." It's just enough information to get the benefit of her help, without having to pull her in to any of the more dangerous stuff.

"Okay," Vanessa says, and I take the book from the shelf. "I'll start with the address."

Silence as she types away. I run my hand over the

cover of the book before opening it to the marked page, not allowing myself any more hesitation than that. On the page are two diagrams of the human skull; one from the front, and one from the side. Illustrations of different types of pliers fill the sides; on the bottom, there are three paragraphs describing the procedure of removing teeth.

Symbolic of life is written in careful handwriting in one of the margins. I recognize Penelope's penmanship immediately. *To take in life is to discover the truth.* Another note closer to the bottom of the page, this one sloppier and more hurried than the rest, reads: *thirty-two teeth per adult.*

I close the book and slide it back on the shelf right away, terrified at the idea of confronting Penelope about what I know once she's awake again but desperate to know what her explanation will be.

"Hey," Vanessa says. "I know this isn't what you're looking for, but I thought it might be cool to see. It's a picture of your family from a long time ago."

I leave the nonfiction section behind to go see what she's talking about, grateful to get away from *A Guide To Post-Mortem Examination.* As I reach the computer, I can see an article on the screen about some celebration for the estate. *HISTORICAL LANDMARK COMES UNDER NEW OWNERSHIP*, the headline reads. I stare with my heart in my throat at a photo of my mother, Eva, hugely pregnant with me and standing beside my father, in the front of the house, along with about twenty other club members. Penelope stands in the back, looking at the camera with lifeless, disdainful eyes. This must have been taken when she still lived in her little apartment in town with baby Margaret.

Vanessa backs out of the article to continue scrolling down the list, which is packed full of irrelevant headlines. I remember Margaret telling me that our mothers hated each other, how badly Penelope wanted to be the head of the estate.

"Hey..." Vanessa says as her eyes light up with the reflection of the screen. "Check this one out."

I look to find a news article that is much, much older than the ones from the first few pages. *HOME FOR ABANDONED YOUTH OPENS AFTER LAND BOUGHT OUT,* the headline screams across the top of the page. Accompanying the article is a dark, grainy photograph of the estate.

In the background of the photo is the house, but I hardly recognize it. Instead of tile roofing, the top of the place is covered with long boards of wood that stick out jaggedly over the edges of the walls. The courtyard is nothing but an open field of weeds and bushes, and the iron gate surrounding the perimeter of the garden is gone. The driveway is a wide dirt path. The stone walls are the only things that look the same.

Standing in front of the house is a large group of people in dated clothing, most of them younger, their expressions solemn. "What year was this taken?" I wonder aloud.

"1899." Vanessa scrolls down to read the caption beneath the photo. "'Founder Clara Owens stands with her students and newly hired staff, shortly after the opening of the home.'"

I look over the faces of the students, fascinated at the sight of them. Is that why there are so many bedrooms in the house? Because it was built to be a home for abandoned youth? A woman who I assume is the founder, Clara, stands to the side of the group while the rest of the staff lines the back. Her chin is pointed proudly upward; she is wearing a long black dress and elaborate matching hat. Strings of pearls hang around her neck.

I skim the article eagerly, disappointed when I don't find anything too worthy of note. The woman was from out of country; she bought the property; she opened the home. While my gut tells me it's relevant in some way, there isn't enough here to make any direct connections. "I wonder what would happen if we did a search for Clara's name?"

We try it. The only results that come up are the one we already saw about the opening and an obituary printed in 1903. "Only four years after opening the place," Vanessa says. "And she was just thirty-three when she died. So young."

"It doesn't mention how she died." I lean forward

to scan the column of text. "Just that she passed away at home surrounded by those she loved most."

"Look here," Vanessa says, pointing at the screen. "It says 'Ms. Owens was laid to rest on the property, the place she felt most at home. Her staff insisted that it was the only appropriate place for a woman who dedicated her life to helping her students.'"

"The cemetery," I say, chilled at the idea of the woman in the picture being buried in the woods outside the house, forgetting that I wasn't going to mention any of this to Vanessa. "Maybe that tomb is hers. But what about all the other graves?"

"What is it with all the talk about the graves?" Vanessa says, leaning back in her seat. "I'm glad for your sake that you missed out on the scene Penelope made when she first got back last night, but the things she was saying were messed up. She mentioned a graveyard in the woods, just like you did. So what's going on, Lucy?"

"Penelope mentioned the graveyard?" I ask, forgetting for a moment about the article. "What did she say?"

"Stuff." Vanessa raises a brow. "But you need to answer my questions first."

I know I should lie to her, but more and more I realize that I don't really want to. After everything that's happened, I want someone to share this with, because doing it all by myself is too hard. I remember the razor in the bathtub, how I'd given up, what happened when I tried to follow through with it. *Just leave the part out about hearing Margaret and Eva in the walls.*

"After Penelope went missing, Margaret and I took a walk through the woods to see if we could find anything," I explain, avoiding Vanessa's eye. "We found this cemetery, although it wasn't like a real cemetery because there was no gate or any kind of separation at all. There were just gravestones in random spots among the trees."

"And you said there was a tomb, too?" Vanessa asks. "Man, that's just weird."

I imagine Penelope digging up the graves, pulling the teeth from the corpses.

"Margaret freaked out when she saw it," I say, my chest tightening at the memory. "I mean, she *really* freaked out. And then, the night she died, remember how we couldn't find her anywhere?"

"Yes," Vanessa says, like she isn't sure she wants to know what comes next. Too late for that. I'm not sure I could stop now, even if I wanted to.

"I saw her coming back from the woods through the library window," I continue. "I saw her flashlight as she ran. When she came back in through the kitchen, she told me she'd gone back to the cemetery."

"And then…she killed herself," Vanessa says slowly.

"Yeah," I say, wishing more than anything that as soon as I'd seen Margaret that night, I'd tackled her, held her down, screamed for help and refused to let go until someone took us both far away from the estate. "So between that and the fact that Penelope apparently mentioned it," I continue, "I thought it might be worth looking into, although I don't understand why yet." I look to the article again. "Can you please tell me what it was that she said last night?"

Vanessa nods, the corners of her mouth turned down. "She was rambling about the graveyard in the trees," she says. "Asking why nobody had ever properly used it, to get to a place much better than this. She wasn't making any sense."

A place much better than this.

Free us or join us.

"Wait." Vanessa stares into my face, her expression hard to read. "Are you saying you think there's something unnatural happening here?"

I think of Margaret knocking on the wall in the attic, her hair dirty with dark circles under her eyes. I think of when she told me that she was being haunted. I think of when I heard her voice in the walls after she died, telling me she was hurting, begging me to help her.

"No," I say. It's hard to tell if Vanessa believes me. "I just think there has to be a connection of some kind, that's all."

"Let's just say this graveyard had something to do with Margaret killing herself," Vanessa says. "Then why would you want to get caught up in something like that?"

Because I have to, I want to say. *Because if there's a way to free Margaret's soul, I have to make sure it happens.*

"Because I want to understand what happened." I look back to the computer screen, where a picture of Clara Owens stares back beside the column containing her obituary. "And I want to know where my aunt has been and what's wrong with her."

"I don't like this," Vanessa says, her tone flat. "I don't like this at all."

"Me, either." I reach to grab the computer mouse, exit the screen and stand from the black leather library chair. "Welcome to the club."

"It's definitely disturbing," she says, standing, as well. "But all of it can be explained by one thing or the other. You do know that, right?"

She seems tense when I don't answer right away. "It's unfair, of course," she continues. "But not like that ever matters in life. Still, I wish you weren't going through all of this."

I think of when I first saw Vanessa, standing in the dining room with wet hair and a stupid grin. Maybe in a different life we could have been friends.

"Thanks," I say awkwardly, and we start to head out. "I just need Penelope to wake up enough to actually talk to me about where she's been, and what's going on with that place."

"I'm sure she will." Vanessa stretches and takes a deep breath through her nose. "In the meantime, though, maybe you should get some sleep yourself. You don't look so good."

I hold off on telling her that I didn't sleep last night. "Thanks?" I say and smile despite myself. The smile fades when I realize that Margaret looked like she could use some sleep, too, shortly before she died. "Anyway, see you later."

"Yep," Vanessa says, heading down the hall to the stairs. "Tomorrow is the big day, huh?"

At first I don't get it. "Big day?"

She looks over her shoulder now, as if worried. "Tomorrow's your family's holiday party, remember?"

I didn't remember, actually, and if she never reminded me just now I probably would have forgotten until people started arriving. I cannot believe we're going on with the party after Penelope's return.

"Oh, yeah," I say. "That big day."

"It's a big day for me, too," Vanessa says, pausing at the top of the stairs. "It means I finally get to leave this place. No offense, but I think my mom has literally lost her mind over the planning for this thing. Nothing's worth that."

I realize that I never asked her how Miranda was doing since our talk in the courtyard, when I found her crying. It reminds me of the mistake I always made with Margaret—forgetting to care because I was too zoomed in to my own problems, leaving us both alone. "No offense taken," I say after a moment, but she's already gone.

Once I'm alone, the weight of nervousness and fear and dread comes back to me like it never left. I go back to my bedroom to sit on the bed that I've pulled to the middle of the room, afraid at first that I'll hear more voices, but I'm only able to sit for about thirty minutes before I fall into a deep sleep.

I wake with a start, unsure if I really just heard someone say my name or if it was part of a dream. It's almost dark, and the house is dead silent. I look around my room for a second before scrambling out, terrified of hearing the voice of Margaret or my mother. She only spoke a few sentences to me, but the idea that she's watching me now is devastating. What if... What if Penelope *murdered* her? To get control of the estate? I shake my head to get the thought out. If there was ever a time for faith, it's now. And I know in my heart that my aunt is not a murderer.

I just do.

The entry room is already partly decorated for the party tomorrow. Long stretches of evergreen garland are draped in graceful swoops around the top perimeter. White string lights drip from the walls below them. Unlit red, white and gold candlesticks sit embedded in the holders around the room, their wicks soft and new. Gold star ornaments hang suspended from different lengths of clear plastic thread that connect to the ceiling. Miranda and Vanessa must have done it while I was asleep.

Curious, I go through to Penelope's door, listening in but hearing nothing. Is she still sleeping? I crack the door open just a bit to peek inside, only to find the bed empty and remade. The room has been cleaned up. The large black leather bag the nurse was carrying is gone, as is the plastic container he dropped the empty syringe into.

There's no sign my aunt was ever here.

"Dad?" I call, my heart racing, as I run into his study. It's empty, as well. Is it possible they finally had to take her to the hospital? Did things get worse after I left?

Suddenly I hear someone shuffling down the grand staircase in the entry room, just as I reach the hall and step in. It's my father, looking exhausted and a bit disheveled.

"Where's Penelope?" I blurt out. "I just went to her room to check in on her and she's gone."

"Penelope requested to be moved out of that room," my father says. "She couldn't stand how the sun was coming in through the windows. It was hurting her eyes."

"There are blinds," I say. "Why didn't you close them?"

"There were other things she didn't like about staying there," my father snaps, clearly drained of all patience.

"For one, she accidentally saw that drawer of photographs that Margaret had ruined, and wasn't *that* fun, trying to find a simple way to explain it to her when she can't even remember who Margaret is in the first place. She thought the pictures were real, that her face really was just a mess of black scribbles. It set her off again."

"So where is she now?" I ask. "Don't tell me you put her in Margaret's room."

"I thought about it," my father says, "but she specifically requested to stay in the attic."

NINETEEN

"WHAT?" I STARE UP at him in disbelief. "Why would you put her in the attic? There isn't even a bed up there, or a bathroom, and how could you let her stay where Margaret...where she..."

"Margaret didn't kill herself in that room," my father argues. "She died in the garden. The cover on the window has been bolted permanently shut."

I am so tired of his bullshit. I know he's involved in this in some way—he has to be! I think back to everything I've seen from him since Penelope disappeared. He seemed anxious and worried while she was gone, like he truly missed her, but it wasn't like he was actually *grieving*. And I'm still not sure that he ever actually called the police—between that and the fact that he didn't force her to go to a regular hospital once she returned, it's obvious he knows whatever it is she's been up to.

If only I was able to tell him about what I've seen, what I've heard, what I know. If only I hadn't backed down when Margaret threatened to tell my father about my glittery, bejeweled box. I think of that box with longing now, even though I know it's wrong. If it wasn't for Margaret's trapped soul, I'd probably be dead by now, anyway, so what harm could come from thinking of that box like you would a childhood blanket? My father would be humiliated if he found out.

"It's safe, don't worry," he continues. "Howard and I were able to get a twin bed up there from one of the spare rooms without too much of a ruckus. And your aunt is fully capable of going down the stairs to use the bathroom on the third hall."

"And all that trouble for what?" I demand, still unable to handle what I'm hearing. "To humor a woman who doesn't even remember her own daughter but wants to sleep in the room where Margaret's last days were spent? That's so sick, Dad!"

"If we want her to recover, we have to help her how we can," my father says. "Penelope wanted to be moved up. She asked about it again and again, and if it will help her get better, why not? Accommodations can be made. Anything to get her back to her old self. Also, the winter holiday party is tomorrow and you know how we like to use the parlor. We wouldn't want—"

"Oh, wow," I cut him off, my anger doubling. "You just wanted her out of the way for your stupid little *club party*? 'Carol of the Bells' doesn't sound quite as lovely when there's a madwoman babbling on in the next room over, is that right? You wouldn't want the club to see their queen in ruins."

"Watch what you're saying," my father says, his face reddening. "Do not insult me or question my motivations. That is unfair. How do you think Penelope would feel if there were people coming in every minute to gawk at her while the party was going on? This isn't a zoo. She isn't an animal to be gawked at. She should be allowed to come back to herself, come back to *us*, in peace. On her own terms."

His eyes have glazed over, and I would feel a little bit guilty for going off on him so hard if it wasn't for the fact that I know he's hiding stuff from me, important stuff, dangerous stuff. Still, it's the only thing he's said that has made even a little bit of sense, even if he doesn't understand how messed up it is for my aunt to move into the attic.

I don't know this on any certain terms, but it's something I can feel deep down, an understanding so solid it nearly launches me into a fit of tears.

"Sorry," I mumble and step around him onto the steps. "I need to leave now."

"Lucy." He sounds remorseful as I leave him behind.

I stop on the stairs and look back. "What?"

"You don't look so well," he says. "I'm…worried. About you. Is there anything you'd like to talk about?"

The grandfather clock in the entry goes off. The whimsical tune that precedes the gongs echoes loudly off the tile and walls and shelves made of glass. We wait for it to pass as he peers up at me, almost like he's looking for something specific.

"Where was this type of concern when I told you that Margaret wasn't doing well?" I ask when the clock has stopped chiming. "Maybe you could have made a difference then, but it's too late to try now." It's painfully similar to what Margaret said to me when I tried to ask her what was wrong, and I think to myself, *this is what a cycle feels like.*

His mouth twitches. "I'm doing the best I can," he says. "I just want everyone to be okay, and for this nightmare to end. And it will," he adds. "You just need to trust us."

There it is. He does know something; he just expects me to sit back, do nothing and accept it.

"If you don't mind," I say coldly, "I need to talk to Penelope."

I leave my father behind without another word, aware as I go up the stairs that he is watching me.

I find my aunt in the attic, sitting up in bed, which has been set up between the wooden wall Margaret used to knock on and the one with the enormous window that she jumped out of. All of the boxes that used to be piled in the back of the room are now neatly stacked to form a wall in front of the closed window covering. At least it's blocked where I can't see it.

"My father wanted to know if you could meet him in the garage," I tell Howard after I've finished climbing up through the opening on the floor, knowing fully well that my father never goes in the garage. "He needed to ask you something about my aunt's treatment plan."

"I just spoke to him fifteen minutes ago," Howard says, irritation lacing his voice. "What could he have forgotten already?"

"I think he just had a few more questions." I look at Penelope as I say it. She looks back, shoots me a weak grin, but her eyes are shining and wide.

"All right," Howard says. "I'll be back shortly, Penelope. For the time being, please remain in bed."

"Thank you, Howard," she says, her eyes still on mine. The nurse in the houndstooth suit saunters past me to climb down the miniature staircase that leads to the third floor.

"Lucy," my aunt says, her voice much clearer than the last time we spoke. "I've been waiting and waiting for you to wake up and come see me."

How is it that she remembers me but not Margaret? I don't rush to her side this time, don't grab her hand and nearly start crying over how much I missed her.

Her hair is clean, combed into a side braid that rests like a snake over her shoulder.

"Where have you been all this time?" I say, taking a step forward. "Do you have any idea what's been happening since you left?"

Her face dims at my tone. "Some things I know better than others," she answers, speaking carefully. "But I do know that the future is bright."

"Why do you swallow teeth?" I burst, unable to keep it in a second longer. "Tell me what kind of witchcraft you've been doing, and who the Mother is, and why you don't know who Margaret—"

My aunt's hands fly over her ears, and she starts shaking her head viciously from side to side. "Don't talk about Margaret," she nearly growls, her eyes clenched shut. "Please, I'm begging you…"

I don't want to waste the precious time alone I've secured with my aunt, and there's so much to ask. I decide to humor her and move on, but in my head I've decided: *it's not that she doesn't remember Margaret, it's that she feels too guilty about what happened to her to face it.*

"I won't talk about Margaret," I promise, nervous that I'll run out of time, but terrified that her display means there isn't a way to free my cousin's soul, as well as the soul of my mother and whoever else is trapped in there. "But please, you need to tell me what's going on."

"Your father said you've been asking about the club,"

she says, slowly lowering her hands from her ears. "He said you know about how they want to take this place away from us."

"Only because you were gone, though," I answer. "They just didn't want Dad to have it, but they love you."

"Or so they say." Her eyes narrow in the slightest as her hands start wringing over each other, as if she's washing them. "But they've been after the grounds for years, and ever since Gregory caught me serving the Mother, he's threatened to expose me, humiliate me into giving up my position—"

"That's it?" I ask, throwing my hands in the air. "*Those* are the *circumstances* that gave them pull over us? That doesn't mean anything! They wouldn't be able to do *anything*. The law doesn't care about..."

I can't even go on any further, I'm too upset. There is no real threat in that stupid club, no magical danger, nothing but the never-ending scramble for money and prestige. Penelope has been doing all this weird ritualistic stuff on her own.

"I don't care about me," Penelope nearly snarls, as if the answer is obvious. "It's the Mother that cannot be exposed. She must be protected, as she's protected me. The best thing for you to do is stay out of the way and let this happen. Tomorrow we'll show him."

Tomorrow is the holiday party. Has this been one big plan from the start?

"What are you going to do?" I ask. "Penelope...
who is the Mother?"

"Giver of the divine, maker of the great," my aunt
responds, and I feel sick to my stomach to hear her talk
like that. How did she hide it so well before everything started to go wrong? Maybe she didn't. Maybe
Margaret was only seeing the obvious, and I was too
in denial to realize that Penelope isn't a perfect, loving parent. I just wanted her to be, needed her to be.
She was all I had.

And look at her now.

I remember what I found in the library and find
the need to ask her about it before Howard gets back;
surely by now he has realized my father isn't coming
to meet him. If I mention Margaret again, she might
get set off. Even now she looks on the brink of madness, sitting forward in the bed, wringing her hands
while her eyes are open wide and her mouth pulled
into a tight-lipped grin.

"If you serve Her, She will take care of you forever,"
Penelope continues. "And tomorrow She'll make sure
certain members of the club find it in their best interest to leave us, and the estate, alone."

"But I don't want her to take care of you, if she's the
one causing people to die around here. Walter, and..."
I pause before saying Margaret's name. "I think you
know who else."

"Sometimes, people get into things that they

shouldn't," Penelope says simply, although she looks disturbed at her own words. "The knowledge drives them mad. That's all. That's why you need to stay away now. You've come too close."

"But I've heard things," I argue. "There are voices of dead people inside the walls, Penelope, and did you know that this house used to be a home for abandoned youth?"

My aunt looks right at me then. "Clara's school," she nearly whispers. "Yes, I did."

"You know who Clara Owens is?"

"She is the one who first brought the teachings of the Mother," Penelope says. "She shared what she knew with an ancestor of ours. The knowledge was passed down through the generations, to anyone who wanted to hear it. Your mother sure didn't."

I think of Eva's voice in the wall with Margaret's. "Penelope," I say slowly. "What happens if you make the Mother angry?"

My aunt nearly shrivels into herself, pulling her knees to her chest and wrapping her arms around them to rock back and forth. "You don't," she says. "You can't."

That just about tells me all I need to know. "You're going to end up getting yourself killed," I say. "And who knows who else."

"No," she insists. "You just need to trust me, Lucy.

How did you come to stop trusting me with such
ease?"

"Because you disappeared and I thought you were
dead!" I bellow. "And then I had to watch Margaret's
head explode on a fence after she thought you were
talking to her from beyond the grave!"

She flinches violently at my words, but it's hard to
care anymore. I got my answers, but I don't like them.

"Make the Mother release the spirits trapped inside
the walls," I command, and my aunt whimpers. "They
shouldn't have to be trapped in eternal darkness and
pain because you're serving some demon woman in ex-
change for...whatever it is you're getting, if anything."

"In return, I receive strength," she says, "and pro-
tection, and eternal love."

"You couldn't have just found Jesus, for Christ's
sake?"

I hear footsteps below me suddenly—Howard returning from downstairs. I have to hurry.

"Please tell me there's a way to free them," I plead.
"Tell me that it's an accident that they're there, that
you didn't put them there. I know you don't want to
hear it anymore, but Margaret was your *daughter*, Penelope, and she's suffering..."

"We can talk about it after the holiday party," my
aunt promises shrilly, her eyebrows pulling together in
frustration. "Just please, trust me enough to wait that
long. Promise me you won't interfere..."

My dad told me that Penelope wouldn't be actually attending the party, so what will she be doing instead? What grand gesture or threat can be made if she's not even there to do it?

"Funniest thing," Howard says, his head suddenly appearing through the hole on the floor behind me. "He wasn't there."

"Strange." My tone is flat. I am still staring at Penelope as he scrambles the rest of the way up the staircase from below. "Do you promise what you said? After the holiday party we can—"

"Yes, yes," Penelope interrupts, clearly not wanting to talk about any of this in front of Howard. "Find me when it's over, and you'll be glad you did."

"We'll see about that," I say, turning my back on her and almost walking straight into Howard.

"Sorry," I mumble. "My father probably changed his mind."

"I'm sure," Howard says, one eyebrow cocked. He doesn't look pleased in the slightest, or like he believes me.

I leave without a goodbye to Howard or my aunt. The sun has gone down by now, and the house is dark except for the light coming from my father's study on the first floor. After thinking about it for a few seconds, I get off the stairs on the second floor, but instead of going to my own room, I go straight into

Margaret's for the first time since I found the picnic basket in the closet.

Without hesitation, I tear down all the stuff on her closet shelf, then lift myself back up just long enough to crawl forward in the darkness, my hand outstretched, until I reach the picnic basket. I shove it aside to grab the shining black wallet behind it. There are no whispers coming for me this time, telling me how much it hurts to be dead; maybe the voices know I no longer care if it hurts. It cannot possibly hurt more than this.

Let's see if I can get Margaret to come out now, I think, so I can tell her that I'm close, so very close, to finding out how to free her. But when I take the wallet to the bathroom where I last heard the voices and open it up wide, take out the scalpel and lower it over the skin on my leg, nothing happens.

I make one small cut, just to see. It takes a bit to start bleeding.

Nothing.

I make another cut, which bleeds much easier than the first.

"Margaret," I say through gritted teeth. "Are you there?"

Then, after a pregnant pause: "Mom?" The word feels like the most unnatural thing I've ever said.

But there are no voices. For now, I am alone.

I cry myself to sleep in the tub, my leg still bleeding, my fingers wrapped loosely around the cool metal handle of the scalpel. In my dreams, Margaret's voice begs me to kill myself, to join her at last, to forget about waiting for the holiday party just to fulfill some empty promise to a crazy woman.

Join me, I can hear her saying, over and over and over again. *You know you want to.*

TWENTY

WHEN I WAKE UP, the scalpel and the wallet are gone.

No matter who it is that came and found me in here, it means I'm ruined. Somebody knows.

The bathroom door is slightly ajar. I close it, lock it and immediately start the shower, hardly able to stand the sight of the dried blood on my leg. *I was just trying to make Margaret appear,* I tell myself. *That's all.*

When I don't feel calmer after a few minutes of standing underneath the stream of water, I crank the temperature almost as high as it will go. I wait until my skin is red and the room is so thick with steam I can feel it entering my lungs with every breath. When I finally step out and wrap a thick towel around myself, I decide I have to know if it was my father who found me in here all cut up with a scalpel in my hands. I'll know immediately if it was him.

I reluctantly get dressed before heading downstairs to his study, which is empty. I check his bedroom, the library and finally the courtyard, even though by then I know I'm grasping for straws. With every room I pass, my chest gets increasingly heavy.

After I've checked all those places, I find Miranda in the dining room with Vanessa, arranging center-pieces down the long table that is draped with gold cloth. Vanessa makes a point to ignore my presence, but I'm here to speak to her mother, anyway.

"Do you know where my father is?" Miranda looks beyond high-strung. I remember again what Vanessa said about her mother being spread too thin at this job, something that is painfully obvious in the messiness of her hair and the shadows beneath her eyes. I swallow my concern—I don't have time to be worrying about Miranda right now.

"Yes," she mumbles, straining to lean across and straighten the tablecloth where it got rumpled from the centerpiece. "He said he had some things to take care of before the big night. Left early this morning."

She doesn't look at me as she speaks. Vanessa looks worried about it for a moment, but when she sees me noticing, she looks away again.

"If you see him before I do, could you please tell him I'm looking for him?"

Miranda doesn't answer, just keeps adjusting the centerpieces before turning toward Vanessa. "I'm going to take you to the bus stop so you can go into town and get the rest of the supplies from the list," Miranda tells her daughter, still ignoring me. "It'll take you most of the day, but that's all right. I'll be able to prepare the turkeys and get them into the ovens without too much hassle."

"Are you sure, Mom?" Vanessa says. "Before we went to bed last night, you said you needed more help here."

"I've changed my mind," Miranda snaps, then makes her way to the edge of the room, where she readjusts candles that were straight in the first place. "Go get your coat and your purse. The list is on the desk in my bedroom."

Vanessa leaves the room, her eyes on the floor as she walks past me. Miranda follows her.

"If you see my father," I say after them, "please tell him to find me right away."

"Okay," I hear Vanessa say right before they exit the room. I wonder if that means that she doesn't hate me, but probably not. She's probably beyond freaked out about all the stuff with the graveyard and Clara Owens. Maybe it wasn't such a great idea to have her help me, after all.

Or maybe it was her *that found you this morning. Or Miranda.*

Riddled with nervous paranoia, I spend the rest of the

morning wandering the grounds, waiting impatiently
for my father to get back from wherever he is. He still
isn't back by the time I need to start getting ready for
the holiday party. If I can't find him beforehand, I'll
have to pull him aside at dinner.

From the courtyard, I look into the woods and bite
my lip and wonder just what in the hell is out there,
but more important, *why*. I think back to all the things
Penelope said about the Mother—that she was loving,
protective, divine—but feel doubtful as I remember
that poem I found in the attic when I was ten. I remember the Mother of the poem being terrifying,
melodies of screams and whatever else.

I make my way back around the front of the house
from the courtyard. I'm rounding the corner where
the driveway swirls around the fountain when I hear
the unfamiliar sound of a buzz saw whirring loudly
from inside the garage. Sometimes my father will hire
a small team of carpenters to come make custom bars
or archways to drape with flowers, to more intimately
customize the bigger parties.

When I try to open the side door to ask anyone if
they've seen my father, I find that it's locked. I pound
on the door with my fist, but the sound of the saw is
too loud to get through to whoever is working it.

Accepting defeat, I go back inside and drop into the
kitchen for a quick drink of water. Inside the refrigerator are five raw turkeys, prepped and rubbed with

herbs and stuffed with handfuls of velvety-looking black truffles. Shouldn't these be in the oven by now if they're going to be ready for tonight? I hope Miranda didn't lose it completely and blank out on the dinner, for her sake. After all the work she's put into the party, she would probably never forgive herself.

I briefly consider finding Miranda and offering a gentle reminder, but what do I know about cooking turkeys? That, and I couldn't care less about the satisfaction of the club or the party in general, except for the fact that afterward I'll hopefully know if it's possible to free Margaret and my mother.

By the time I'm finished with my shower, the halls are starting to become fragrant with the smell of roasting meat. It saddens me to think that Penelope would usually be hustling all throughout the house before such a party, preparing the guest rooms in case anybody drank too much or going over the music list for the hundredth time to make sure it was exactly how she wanted.

I shake the thought from my head and concentrate on what I'll say to my father when I finally see him while I roll my hair into curlers and put on makeup. I should just say hello or pretend to have a question about Penelope and study how he holds himself around me. If it was him, he won't be able to hide his emotions. And what if that happens? I swallow hard, staring at my reflection, unblinking. *Don't get too ahead of yourself. It could have been someone else—how often has he ever come to check on you himself instead of sending someone?*

At least if it was Vanessa, she's leaving in the morning. I'll never have to see her again.

When I open my closet, I choose the first dress I see, one of rich emerald color and cap sleeves of black lace. I grab my black tights from where they hang over the rack, not caring that there's a run in them. Once I've finished pulling the dress over my head and have stepped into my shoes, I go to my window and peek outside. Sure enough, there are already five or six cars parked in the driveway, on the cobblestone that surrounds the fountain. Their spotless chrome bumpers glow orange from the sunset.

What exactly do Penelope and my father have planned for the club tonight?

In a minute I'm standing on the grand staircase, looking down over the herd of club members as they eat appetizers and make each other drinks at the bar. Still no sign of my father anywhere. I sigh in frustration as I make my way down the steps. The last thing I feel like doing right now is putting on a fake smile for these people through cocktail hour.

"Darling," Nancy Shaw nearly shouts when she notices me stepping off the bottom of the stairs. "Your dress is to die for!"

"Thank you," I say without smiling, walking past Nancy, past the group she's with, all the way to the back of the room where the hallway to the study is. As I pass the appetizer table, I see Gregory Shaw talking in hushed tones with Howard, Penelope's nurse.

"Where's my aunt if you're here?" I ask, ignoring Gregory's cold stare when he notices that I'm here. "Is my father sitting with her?"

Howard lifts an eyebrow as he takes a drink, shooting Gregory a skeptical glance. "We thought maybe you could tell us."

"What?"

"Are you unaware of the current circumstances?" Gregory asks. "How is that even possible? You live here."

"What circumstances?" I ask, my heart rate rising. I can see from where I stand that the light in my father's study is off. "What are you talking about?"

"Your father's gone," Gregory says simply, taking an uneasy sip of drink. "And Penelope, as well."

His words echo in my mind. *Gone.* I feel my breath escape me.

"It's been suspected that they've run off together," Howard says. "Your father said he couldn't handle the pressures of running the estate in coordination with the club anymore."

"*What?*" No. He wouldn't do that. "Who said they suspected that? Are they both really gone?"

"It was your lovely cook, Miranda." Gregory looks over the table of appetizers but doesn't take anything.

"She told us shortly after we arrived this evening. I'm surprised you're still here. Why wouldn't they have taken you with them? Aren't you under eighteen still?"

I can hear my own pulse. "Dinner is being served!" I hear Vanessa's voice call from the entrance of the dining room far behind me, which is followed by the sound of the crowd eagerly making their way in.

My father and Penelope are gone. It could be so many different things, each and every one of them horrible, and this is it, I've run out of time, this is the end of everything.

"Are you all right, Lucy?" Howard steps forward and takes me by the shoulder. "You look like you're about to faint."

It's a genuine struggle to breathe normally. I bring my hands to my face, as if hiding from the two old men will make me disappear. At least everybody else in the room is too busy making their way in to dinner to notice that I'm about to lose my shit.

"Whoa." Gregory quickly sets his martini glass down and reaches forward to help steady me. "You really didn't know, did you?"

Why wouldn't Miranda have told me if they were missing, or if my father had said he was taking Penelope and leaving me? Nobody's come for me all day, the party has been set up and put into motion regardless and now dinner's even been called. I think back to how distant and cold Miranda was when I asked her about my father this morning. Why didn't Vanessa come tell me? That's something she would have done, I feel like, even if we aren't on the best terms. She would have known that I deserve to be told, like when Penelope returned.

Something is terribly, terribly wrong.

"Let's go sit down and have a meal," Howard coaxes as I calm my breathing and straighten up on my own. "We can help you get into contact with anybody you need, police, other relatives…"

"I don't have any other relatives," I say blankly, *except for my dead cousin and mother, whose souls are trapped in the walls.* My head is still a little light as I turn to spot Vanessa, who watches me intently from the entrance to the dining hall. I walk away from Gregory and Howard and go straight to her.

"I'm so glad to see you," she says before I can open my mouth. Her hands are clutched together over her stomach. "We need to talk, like, now."

"I was gonna say the same thing." I follow her into the entry hall, where rows of fur coats hang like dead dogs on hooks. "What is going on right now? My father and Penelope are *gone*?"

"What?" Vanessa blurts, her eyes watering. "I don't know anything about your father or Penelope, Lucy, but something's wrong with my mom."

My stomach drops. "What do you mean?"

"I only just got back from taking care of the stuff from that list she made me," she says, looking over my shoulder to the dining room door. "All the time I was out, I kept thinking that it was stuff we'd already done, or stuff we didn't need to do, and I couldn't help but feel like she just did it to send me away for the day. Ever since I got back, she's been different. She kept telling me not to go into the kitchen, not to help with the food until we were out there and it was time to serve..."

Vanessa is cut off by the sound of several startled screams coming from the dining room, mixed with violent gagging noises that echo off the walls and white marble tile. We both take off running for the door instantly, Vanessa crying out for her mom.

We both stop when we can see inside the dining room, about five paces from where the open doorway lies ahead of us. Taking slow, careful steps forward, Vanessa raises her hands to her mouth as if she's going to vomit, while my mouth drops more and more with every moment. At the tables, club members sit in their chairs, recoiling with looks of disgust and horror at what lies on the silver platters before them.

A human leg, the skin split from the heat of the oven as disturbingly pink muscle shines through from beneath. An arm, bubbled and darkened with the fingers curled unnaturally tight. An entire, intact rib cage with the lungs still inside, draped with coils of intestine and surrounded by greens.

On the center platter rests a head, one that I immediately recognize as my father.

TWENTY-ONE

MY MIND GOES back to when I heard the power saw in the garage earlier, and how I became confused at the raw turkeys in the refrigerator. The turkeys never made it to the oven. They weren't the cause of the roasting meat smell that's been thickening the air of the house for hours, after all.

My father's hair is still combed to the side. His mouth is open and filled with a bread stuffing of some sort, which overflows onto the platter that the head rests sideways on. His eyes are sewn closed.

My knees give out and I fall onto my hands, the marble tile cold and gritty beneath them. My breath is heaving; I'm struggling not to pass out. "No," I try to yell, but it comes out like a strangled cry instead.

"Everybody eat up while it's hot," Miranda's voice calls from somewhere hidden from view around the corner, closer to where the entrance to the kitchen is. "Your host wouldn't want anybody to go home hungry."

Cries of disgust and terror erupt from the club members. Miranda killed my father. How, why, *why*? I think of her strung-out appearance, how Vanessa claimed she was acting different, and that she had feelings for my father. She couldn't have done it of her own free will, right? There had to have been something else that caused her to do it. That doesn't change that I'll never see my father again, never struggle to understand what he was thinking, never wonder if he really loved me.

He doesn't love anybody now.

"Oh my God," Vanessa whimpers from beside me. She takes another step forward to the door. "What has she done?"

I hear the sound of a chair scraping across the tile, then Gregory Shaw's voice, shaky but booming. "Stay where you are," he calls to Miranda from across the room. "If you take one more step—"

Vanessa leans down and helps me climb to my feet. We're holding on to each other, keeping each other up, when there comes the earsplitting pop of gunshots, three right in a row followed almost simultaneously by the hard thunk of a body hitting the floor.

"Mom!" Vanessa screams, pulling away from me to tear into the room. I try to grab her shirt, but just like that time in the attic with Margaret, I miss by an inch.

"Don't go in there!" I urge in a loud whisper, but she's already through the doorway. I can't go after her. Not with my dad and Miranda and Gregory Shaw. Penelope has to be around here somewhere. Maybe she's in the attic—that's where she told me to go after the party was over. Miranda was clearly lying when she said my father and aunt had run away together.

Kicking my shoes off so they won't make any noise on the tile, I run to the stairs and start climbing them. I pass the second floor without hesitation, making my way as quickly as possible to the third. Once I reach the top, I turn to make sure nobody's come looking for me yet. The enormous room that looms below is empty. The silence from inside the dining room causes my skin to break out into goose bumps.

I run down the hallway without turning on the lights, then scramble up the miniature staircase below the attic. The single bulb is lit, filling the room with a dim yellow glow, but Penelope's bed is empty.

What could have happened to her? Did Miranda kill her, too, or did she run back to the woods? I nearly throw myself to the floor next to the wall, the same one that Margaret was leaning against before she jumped out the window.

"What am I supposed to do?" I cry out loud, the image of my father's head on a platter still burned in my brain. I should just get out, leave without a word to anybody. If I hurry, maybe I can sneak out through the front door and steal a car from outside.

"Nothing," Margaret's voice comes from behind me, causing me to scream. "You lost the chance to escape what will come now."

A scatter of clicks moves around the surface of the wall from the other side.

"Please," I beg, hitting my hand against the wood. "Penelope promised she'd tell me how to free you! But I don't know where she is, and the police are going to be here soon, and..."

"There won't be any police." Her voice is softening, deepening somehow. I have to lean my ear against the wall to hear her clearly. "And there's no reason for you to try to help free me anymore. My demands have been met by someone else."

"What demands?" I don't like how she sounds, so cold, so different, so unlike my cousin. "Margaret? What happened to your voice?"

"Oh, sweet child," comes the reply. "Over the years, I have become a thing of many voices."

I pull my ear away from the wall quickly, the blood in my face like ice. "Where is my cousin?" I demand, slowly getting to my feet. "Where are Margaret and my mother?"

"They're dead," the voice says simply. "But I know you just as well as they did, if not better. I've been here for a long, long time."

All those times that I thought I was talking to them, how much I missed my cousin, how much I wanted to help her, how I felt when I first heard my mother's voice. It wasn't even them.

"What is happening?" I cry, my hands coming to rest on the sides of my face.

"A growth spurt," the voice says. "Felix's death has completed the spell, and Miranda's, well...Miranda's just added an extra bit of flair, shall we say."

A wave of nausea rolls over me as I realize what the voice is saying: that every death that took place in the house made it stronger somehow. But what is it? More important, what has it grown into?

"I have to say," it continues. "At first you were to just be more fuel for me, more energy, but you never gave in to the madness I instilled, like the others did. There's something...special about you."

So Margaret was manipulated into losing her mind by the voice, which made itself sound like Penelope for her. Then it sounded like Margaret for me. I wonder what Walter heard in the walls, what Miranda heard in order to cut my father to pieces and roast him in the oven.

I take a step backward toward the latched attic door. "What spell?"

"The spell to set me free, of course." There comes a lively series of light taps that dance all over the surface of the wall. "The process of getting revenge on those who put me here. The process of *metamorphosis*, sweetling. My transformation is complete."

With that, there comes a cracking boom so loud that I cry out without meaning to and stumble back, almost falling. Something hits the wall from the other side, hard, then again but even harder.

Boom.

Dust rises from the surface of the wall as it rattles.

Boom.

A small crack awakens down the center of the wood, about two feet high. My breath catches in my throat.

BOOM. The crack deepens and grows vastly in size as splinters of wood are spit forward.

I make a hurried dash to the secured attic door and heave it open, only going down the first few steps before jumping the rest of the way to the third floor. As I hit the ground, I hear an explosion of wood in the attic above me, along with the sound of pieces of the wall skidding across the floor. I stand up and sprint down the hallway to the grand staircase. The entry room is still empty, but I can hear the sound of people talking in hushed, angry tones in the dining room, where my father was served for dinner.

I go down the stairs so fast it feels like I'm gliding, but running across the tile floors with stocking feet proves to be more difficult than I'd wish. I burst into the dining room, not caring if the people inside mean to murder me.

"Where's Vanessa?" I shout at the club members who are still seated around the grisly scene on the table. "What are you all still doing here? We need to get out!"

This is when I realize that even though Gregory Shaw is sitting upright and still in his chair, his throat has been slit. Red soaks the front of his suit, and his eyes are wide-open. Beside him, Kent Dickens sits the same way.

I look slowly to Nancy Shaw, grand, glamorous Nancy Shaw with her brightly painted mouth and love for vodka martinis. She sits beside Kent, very much alive. In fact, all the wives are alive.

"Don't be too frightened, dear," Nancy says, and takes a sip from the wineglass in front of her. She nods to her dead husband. "I killed him myself. He discovered far too much about the true value of this place, beyond the money, thanks to what happened to Felix. And, well..." She drains her glass, looks over at Gregory's body regretfully. "That simply wasn't any of his business."

I'm frozen in place, too scared to move.

"But I would never dream of hurting *you*, of course," she continues when she sees my face. "You're an Acosta."

"There's something coming," I say, my ears buzzing at what she just said. "From the attic, we have to go before it kills us."

"Oh, I'm counting on her to come down." There's a sudden edge to Nancy's voice. I look to count the other women who sit silently with their eyes on mine; there are four of them. "It's her fault that all of this happened, after all. When Penelope first disappeared, we became confused. When Margaret died, we became curious. And when Penelope returned, well..." Nancy takes another sip of her wine. "When she returned, we became suspicious. Enough to send Howard in to keep an eye on things, anyway."

So Howard the nurse was a spy for the club—more specifically, for the club wives.

"Who is she?" My hands are trembling so badly I'm afraid I might lose the ability to use them. "How do you know her?"

"Her name is Clara, dear," Nancy says. "And we're the ones who killed her."

No. "How could you know Clara Owens?" I say in a near whisper. "She died in 1903."

A massively uneasy quiet settles over the room; the calm before the storm.

"I see you've been doing your homework," Nancy says, her fuchsia mouth pulling into a frown. "I sure wish you hadn't done that. It's not that it matters to *me*, but you've been digging into some pretty big stuff. The kind of stuff you wouldn't want to entangle yourself with if you have hopes of ever looking the other way." She sighs. "I'm sure the Mother is well aware of your presence by now."

The Mother. It wasn't just Penelope serving her. *How were these women alive in 1903?*

I brace myself for them to get up and come at me, slit my throat just like they did their apparently disposable husbands, but it would seem that the women have no intention of hurting me. In fact, some of them look into my face with a sort of pained pity, a nostalgia, as if they care about me.

"What about my aunt Penelope?" Penelope was friends with these ladies; all the stress surrounding the club had always seemed to come from the husbands. "Where is she if my father's dead?"

"If she's alive, and something tells me she is," Nancy says, "I'll find her. She was strong, that one. An heir of the sacred grounds, eager to join us. Still, that was before Clara got to her behind our backs, poisoned her mind with whatever lies I can't imagine." She lets out an exaggerated huff, lifts a hand to check her hair. "We could have just *sworn* that bitch was dead!"

The other women nod in agreement. I struggle to keep up: the club wives were secretly a part of some sort of coven that Penelope was joining, a coven that makes you immortal somehow? In the worst way, Margaret would have thought this was hilarious— the women we used to make fun of for their face-lifts and antiaging tactics literally *do not age*. How is that possible?

"Nancy?" a voice calls from the entry room behind me, from somewhere up the stairs. I recognize it immediately as the one from the attic. It's much clearer now that it's not being muffled by the wall, energized and lightened and singsong. The sound of it causes the skin on my back to break into a sweat. "Is that you I hear down there, my love?"

TWENTY-TWO

"IT'S BEST YOU run along now, dear," Nancy says, her voice lost of all frilly charm. "Find your friend in the kitchen and get out. There's more mess ahead and I'm afraid you've seen enough."

The realization is like a punch to the stomach: this is what Penelope had been talking about last night—the reckoning for the *club*. She meant the wives. Why couldn't she have told me that? Did she think I'd try to get involved? Another realization, even worse: she must have known that someone would have to die in order for Clara's transformation to be complete, whatever that means.

We'll show him, she said.

Gregory. She'd said that Gregory had caught her *serving the Mother*, and that the Mother couldn't be exposed. He must have had no idea that his own wife was a follower, too. None of the husbands knew the truth.

The other women sitting around the table rise, anger slowly painting their faces as they step around the table to go into the entryway.

I hurry away in the opposite direction, to the kitchen, where I find Vanessa sitting against the wall with the body of Miranda draped over her lap, bullet wounds over her face and throat and chest. I think of how she sounded when she announced the serving of my father's corpse. I wonder what Clara said to her to push her over the edge into insanity; how many nights she had to keep her awake to string her out enough to go through with it. I wonder whose voice she used when she did it.

"He shot her," Vanessa whispers when she sees me. Her face is streaked with tears, and her eyelids are droopy as if she's drunk. "Then his wife said something about how Clara was back, 'somehow.' The women were upset about it, but the men didn't understand. When they tried asking about it, their wives slit their throats. They all had the same knife."

I remember the blade that I found in the attic when I was ten, with its distinctive curve and handle. *Forget coven*, I think in horror. *It's a fucking cult.*

"I'm so sorry, Vanessa," I say and drop to my knees beside her. "But we have to go now."

"Clara," she answers, still staring into space. "Isn't that the name of the lady we found at the library?"

"Yes," I say and gently pull her out from underneath Miranda's body. The dead woman's eyes are partly open, and her mouth is a mess of blood and meat. "I don't know how or why, but she's been haunting the house. Waiting until there were enough deaths to give her the power to…bust out."

I break into a sweat again. What's Clara doing now? What is she planning? How invincible is she? *Trust me,* Penelope's words echo in my head. *Come find me.*

"That doesn't make sense." Vanessa shakes her head as she looks down at all the blood on her outfit. "None of this does."

A sound rolls in from the parlor: laughter, fast and high-pitched. Clara Owens.

"We can't go through the garage," I say in a mangled whisper, remembering that it was where my father was dismantled. "We'll have to sneak around to the front door."

Vanessa and I move through the dark hallway, the sounds of Nancy and Clara talking closer with each step. I think of when Clara said there was something *special* about me. I don't think I want to know what that means, but at least she isn't aggressively pursuing Vanessa and me. As we round the corner to the entryway that goes into the parlor, I can hear Nancy speaking from the room beyond as we step through the shadows.

"...after all this time."

"Yes, well," the voice of Clara says as Vanessa and I peek around the corner of the hall into the entry room. "I had all the time in the world to figure out how I'd shed enough blood to come back for you," Clara continues. "And like you said—after all this time, here we are!"

As terrified as I am to see Clara in the flesh, I'm too curious not to look.

Nancy Shaw and the four other club wives are gathered on the tile around the base of the grand staircase, looking ridiculous in their elaborate holiday outfits— one woman even wears a tinsel-silver dress with real ornaments on it. About halfway up the steps stands a woman in a black floor-length gown of old Victorian design. Pearls hang in long loops over the front, and a small black hat sits on her head. I recognize her immediately as the woman in the photo from the library.

That's who I've been talking to all this time, the thing that's lurked inside the walls of the house for over a hundred years. There were never any spirits or ghosts, after all. I think of all the things she said to me as Margaret, *stay, you were never there for me, we were best friends until we weren't anymore.* Over the years, Clara didn't just listen to us. She got to know us, too. And she knew all the right things to say to each person to get what she wanted.

"And then?" Nancy says, sounding angry. "You preyed on the newest sister to the coven, and for what? To turn her against us?"

"How does it feel to be betrayed?" Clara nearly spits, losing her composure. "After you tried to end me, you used the sacred grounds but were too afraid to live on it yourselves anymore. You had to set up a steady resident that was at your mercy, is that it? So that just in case I came back, you'd be out of danger?"

"Penelope was a dedicated servant to the Mother," Nancy says, shaking her head stubbornly. "You were no such thing."

"Penelope has her own role to play," Clara states, straightening her back and keeping her voice level. "And the Mother who brings the sanctity to these grounds isn't pleased with you."

"You're wrong," Nancy says, reaching into her holiday dress that's dazzled with red and green sequins and retrieving a small, curved blade—I'm sure it's the knife she used on Gregory, the matching knives that all the women have. "The gift of eternal life has continued to be given with every ritual we do. We are supported."

"Of course you are." Clara takes a step down, then another. "So why do you think the Mother took pity on me, allowed me to be reborn from the ground up, a squirming infant worm inside a magnificent stone cocoon of darkness? Who do you think *processed* the power of those deaths, made them matter in the first place, molded them into what would become my wings?

"I'll give you a hint," she continues. "It's me. You've got your Mother right here."

"These are sacred grounds built to serve the Mother you speak lies of!" one of the women behind Nancy cuts in, pulling out her own blade. The others do the same. "How dare you?"

"This place doesn't belong to you," Clara hisses, bending over a tiny bit at the waist as she cocks her head to the side. "Clara's intuition for the Mother was always the strongest. That's why she was the one to lead you originally. But none of you wanted the truth. Nobody wanted to face that the price for eternal life is death. And when Clara did things right, started sacrificing the students she'd collected in her home here... you all murdered her. You betrayed her. You wanted all the benefits of my power without having to actually earn them."

The price for eternal life is death.

"But...you are Clara!" Nancy says, confused. "Why are you speaking as if you're not?"

"Because I'm the one who found Clara," the woman in the black dress says, her breath beginning to heave. "My precious servant, like a daughter to me, stabbed all over the place and then stuffed into the walls and left to rot. But she was barely alive, and in her last breaths, she whispered to me, called out for me, begged for me to help her."

Nancy's eyes have grown wide in fear.

"So I *became* her," the thing in Clara Owens's body continues. "Let her body evolve and grow into what it is now with the help of my power. Promised her that she would have her revenge, no matter how long it took. Kept you all alive long enough for me to get it for her."

A great rise of sound comes from below the floor-length skirts of Clara's dress, the same echoing skitter that reminds me of the song of cicadas in the summer, the same sound she made one of the first times I heard her inside the walls.

"Which reminds me," Clara says, her smile growing wider and wider. "It's time to pay up for all the years I've lent to you."

The woman who spoke up behind Nancy lets out a frustrated scream and runs toward the woman in the long, black dress. I recognize her now as Kent Dickens's wife.

"Mary-Anne, no!" Nancy cries, keeping her own blade raised.

Before Mary-Anne can slash her little, curved blade across Clara's throat, she is impaled through the center of her face by the black clawed appendage that has risen from beneath the skirts of Clara's dress. It bends in many places, a slithering multi-jointed leg that is riddled with sharp, black quills. A few more of the appendages sprout out from beneath, lifting Clara a few inches off the ground, the pointed toes of her laced boots hovering in midair. Two other appendages uncurl from her back and rise up on either side of her head, the claws at the ends gnarled and shining.

"Oh my God," Vanessa moans from beside me, staggering in place. "Oh my fucking God."

We both fall back a little, although we're far enough away to go unnoticed in the commotion. My instincts urge me to take Vanessa and run out the front door only twenty feet away, leave our parents' bodies behind, leave the estate behind, forever. I stand to do so when I see movement at the top of the grand staircase.

It's Penelope.

TWENTY-THREE

MY AUNT WAVES frantically for me to come up to her, her fingers outstretched, pleading, desperate.

"How do you love your Mother now?" Clara cries in glee as she flings Mary-Anne's body twenty feet across the room, where it collides with the edge of the bar and goes spinning into the wall, blood spreading over the tiles in a spiral design. "Stretching my wings is just as lovely as I imagined it'd be."

The other women let out startled screams and nearly trip over their high heels as they backtrack toward the door that leads to the dining room, leaving a clear path between where I'm standing and the grand staircase.

"It's your aunt," Vanessa says, noticing Penelope now, too, who is still waving wildly. "What is she doing?"

"Calling for me." I look back up at her, the woman

I should hate, the woman who worships the thing that killed Margaret and so many others, my own mother included. I think of her passion when she spoke to me about the Mother in the attic, so very sure everything would be okay. She's been misled. She just needs to be snapped out of it by somebody. "I'm gonna go."

"Are you sure we should go up the stairs?" she whispers, her eyes staying on Penelope. "That doesn't seem like the safest idea."

"Clara has no interest in killing me," I say again, remembering when she told me I was special. "And I never said anything about *we*. You should go out the front door, steal one of the cars in the driveway, drive to town and call 911 as soon as there's service."

"You can't stay," Vanessa begs. "You'll die if you stay, I just know it."

"I won't be able to live much of a life if I run now," I say, the truth evident to me. "I failed Margaret, and I thought I had the chance to redeem that, but it was a lie. I have to go with Penelope, she'll protect me, she *raised* me and…my father loved her."

My words catch in my throat, and my eyes fill with unexpected tears as I think about my father trying to hold everything together with whatever information he did or did not have. I can't help but wonder if Miranda at least knocked him out before sawing him to pieces.

Vanessa hesitates for a moment, her lip trembling as

Clara glides toward the women another few feet. The hum of the insectile buzz radiates through the parlor, along with the sharp clicks of clawed appendages on marble tile. "I...don't want to leave you," she says finally. "We're in this together now. Just as long as you're sure she won't hurt us."

"I don't think she will." I look up at my aunt, still urging me to join her, pointing up even though she's on the third floor. "If the Mother has broken out, there's no more need for more deaths. Plus, she'll never leave this place unless I convince her to."

"Fine," Vanessa mumbles, scratching at the skin on her arms, her eyes still red from crying over her mother. "I don't know how to drive, anyway."

"Me, either," I say, the corner of my mouth turning up ever the slightest. "But don't say I didn't give you the chance to back out if something goes wrong."

We crouch behind an especially tall houseplant while we wait for the room to clear. Nancy is bellowing out instructions as her group is pushed back, but it's doing little use. Clara's top appendage flings across the middle of another club wife's torso, disemboweling her. After a few seconds of shocked gasps, the woman falls into the pile of entrails at her feet.

"Stop this immediately!" Nancy cries. "Clara, I will punish this darkness out of you myself if I have to!"

"Now," I whisper, when the three survivors duck

into the dining room and Clara follows, still making that terrible skittering sound. "Run."

Vanessa and I dash across the tile to the staircase, scrambling up the steps in a beeline for the third floor. "Lucy," my aunt cries out in relief when I've reached her, and she pulls me into a hug. "We need to go, quick. If the passageway has been opened, we are free to use it."

"Passageway?" I ask, but she's already rushing for the back hall, where the entrance to the attic is. "Where are we going? We need to get out of here!"

"There's a hidden way out that you can reach from the attic," she calls back to us. "Nothing can touch us down there."

Down there? But the attic is upstairs.

"Let's just hurry," Vanessa urges me, starting to follow her. "I'll go anywhere that takes me away from that...*thing*."

I hesitate for a moment before making sure that we're not being followed, then dash down the back hallway. In the attic the floor is covered in shards of wood from where the wall was busted out. We wade through the wood pieces to look into the massive hole that was made beside Penelope's bed.

There is a small space, maybe three to four feet wide, in between where the wood of the wall is and where the stone of the exterior wall sits solid and covered in spiderwebs. I stick my head in to see inside. In the back corner of the space, there is a ledge that opens into pitch darkness.

"Follow me," Penelope says, making her way to the ledge. "There's not much time."

"Not much time until what?" I ask, but she doesn't answer. "We can't go in without a light of some kind."

"There's a flashlight in one of the boxes by the window," Penelope says impatiently. "Hurry up if you're going to get it."

Vanessa goes with me to find it. Once we've confirmed the batteries work, we crawl into the space behind the wall.

"What's that sack sitting against the stone?" Vanessa asks, squinting through the shadows as I point the light near our feet. "By where that ledge is."

I point the light at it, the bag resting a few feet in front of Penelope. "This is mine," my aunt says, pleasantly surprised. "I thought I lost it below. The Mother must have saved it for me."

"Below?" I ask, my heart catching in my chest as Penelope swings herself over the side of the ledge. It takes me a few seconds to realize that there must be a ladder there. *To the below.*

"Just follow me," Penelope says and disappears as she starts to climb down. "And leave the bag—I don't need it anymore."

Once she's completely out of sight, I use my fingers sparingly to pick open the top of the burlap sack resting in the back corner against the stone, tilting the light inside so I can peek in. There's nothing inside except for an old knife that I recognize, with a blade covered in dried flakes of blood, and an old photograph, curled at the edges and yellowing in spots over the surface.

It's the same photograph used in that newspaper article we saw in the archives, the group shot with Clara standing in front of her home for troubled youth. I look over the photograph again, understanding how I didn't see Nancy Shaw in it the first time. She looks so different without her painted lips and styled hair. But there she is, sure enough, standing proudly among the other women as a part of Clara's staff—the country club wives.

I slide the knife down the pocket of my dress, deciding not to tell my aunt I have it. *Just in case.*

"I hear someone coming up the stairs to the third floor," Vanessa says in a panic. "We have to get out of here, Lucy. We're going to be killed by that monster..."

"Hurry up!" Penelope's voice echoes from down below. "We're not there yet, but we're close."

I follow Vanessa as she balances herself on the ladder, then begins the climb down. We climb for what feels like forever, the only sounds surrounding us the soft scratching of rat's claws on stone and the steady dripping of water.

All this time, the Mother has lived in the walls of the house, using Clara's body, skittering around and listening and killing with only her words. And Penelope, when she disappeared...where exactly was she? In the walls, too? But I saw her walk into the forest when she disappeared.

Once at the bottom of the ladder, Vanessa flashes the light around us, then up where we just came from to see if anyone is following us. The passageway is clear, for now.

"Where are we?" she says. "I don't think we're in the walls anymore. I think we're beneath the house."

I take the flashlight, and Vanessa links her arm around mine. We're standing in a small stone room that has five different exits placed evenly apart around the perimeter. When I shine the light down them, it is revealed that each exit leads to a vastly long hallway with walls that are made of stone.

"They're tunnels," I say aloud as I realize it, and Vanessa squeezes my arm with hers. "The estate is built over some sort of underground tunnel system."

"Exactly," Penelope nearly whispers. "Do you know how deep some of these go, girls? It's completely magnificent. If the Earth had veins, these would be it."

Beyond the beam of the flashlight, the stone passageways reach into what seems like eternal blackness. It smells musty and dank, and it's freezing cold. I sincerely regret kicking my shoes off in the house earlier. If I'm in here too long, I might lose my toes or feet or worse.

"That one will lead you outside through the empty

tomb in the cemetery," Penelope says, pointing to the tunnel on the far right. "But that's not where we're going tonight. Tonight it's tunnel number three."

"If that one leads out, we should go through it," I argue. "Penelope, I know you love this Mother, but—"

"I hope you're not going to talk badly about Her," she says, her tone low. "If you even knew what She's been through— She's a higher being, but it's not as though Clara is completely dead, either! There is a part of her that's still alive in her new form, all those memories and thoughts and feelings. The Mother feels everything Clara feels, the pain, the anger..."

"But Margaret died because of her," I try, talking as calmly as I can through my chattering teeth.

"I told you not to talk about Margaret," my aunt cries out, her voice bouncing off the stone walls. "The Mother must be allowed to take whatever measures necessary and all I have to do is have faith in Her decisions. No questions asked."

Penelope starts scratching her head sporadically, walking in more exaggerated movements. I think about how filthy Penelope was when she finally returned home, how out of it she was. Howard said that she hadn't slept for days. She wasn't doing a ritual in the tomb, I think. She was wandering these tunnels.

But why? Why would the Mother let her live down here?

The knife rests heavily in my dress. I hope I haven't

made a huge mistake. Vanessa stays close to me, about ten paces behind Penelope. I shine the light back to the front of the tunnel, wanting to run back and choose the one that I know for certain leads out.

"I can't go any farther," I say and stop walking. "I'm going to go out the cemetery and leave this place."

Vanessa lets out a sigh of relief from beside me.

"Don't be ungrateful now, Lucy," Penelope says and stops as well, to turn around. "This is your destiny."

"You said you were leading us out."

"Did I not do that?" my aunt answers, reaching into her pockets. "Don't you want to get away from your life now, Lucy? With everything you've been struggling with, everything that's *wrong* with you?"

She pulls out the black leather wallet from Margaret's room. The one with the scalpel inside. The one that someone took out of my hands when I was sleeping last night. It was Penelope.

"That's not mine," I say right away, despite the stupidity of the statement. I wrap my arms tighter around myself, take a step back, hate myself for not just leaving when I had the chance. *Too late now.* I'm always too late.

"Of course it's not yours," my aunt says, her voice overly warm. "It's mine."

TWENTY-FOUR

THE WALLET DIDN'T belong to Margaret. My cousin never coped the way I did, never counted hidden scars over and over again until the concept of numbers faded away. Even in the awful stone tunnel, the realization warms me, a tiny pardon after a long line of fuck-ups.

"But why was it in Margaret's closet?" I ask, wanting all the proof in the world that the scalpel wasn't Margaret's.

"I hid it in there, along with some other things," Penelope says. "I don't use it in the same way you do, of course." She makes a *tsk tsk tsk* sound with her tongue, like I'm being scolded for stealing a cookie before dinnertime. "I use it for much more practical things."

She takes the scalpel out of the wallet now, flashes

the blade at Vanessa and me. "And I could tell you all about those things, if you'd just come with me now."

She's insane, I realize, and the anger starts to bubble away uncontrollably inside. "You want to talk about faith?" I say, taking just one step forward, and Vanessa reaches out for my arm to stop me from going farther. "Do you realize how much faith I put in you, how many times I've had to give you the benefit of the doubt? In the end, it was for *nothing!*"

Penelope's eyes narrow just a bit. I step back and start making my way toward the other tunnel entrances, Vanessa close behind. "Lucy," my aunt calls. "Come back here right now."

"No," comes my reply. As we make our way through the dark tunnel, I turn back every few seconds with the flashlight to make sure she isn't following us. When we finally step into the open stone room below the house, Nancy Shaw is standing there, shivering and alone.

"Thank God it's you," she gushes at the sight of our faces. "I saw your light coming closer, and I thought maybe Clara had somehow gotten ahead of me..."

"Stay away from us," Vanessa says right away. "We're leaving on our own. If you want to hash things out with Penelope, she's in the middle tunnel. Have a ball." She pulls my sleeve toward the tunnel on the end and we inch away from the woman in the blood-splattered sequined dress.

"My sisters are all dead," Nancy weeps, reaching out

for us. "Please, please don't leave me, take me with you, we'll all escape together. I can pay you any amount of money that you desire. We've accumulated a massive amount over the decades."

So that's where all the money came from. They already had it all saved up, ready to throw around for whatever reason they wanted. No wonder Gregory Shaw *settled* for Nancy over Penelope. The woman was filthy rich.

"No, thanks," I say, removing the knife from the pocket of my dress and pointing it at Nancy. "Stay away from us so I don't have to use this, please."

Vanessa suddenly stops dead, causing me to bump into her from behind. "Why did you stop?" I ask hurriedly, keeping my eye on Nancy.

"Because there's something standing in the doorway," comes the horrified reply.

"Excuse me," Clara's voice says from the darkness in front of the last tunnel. Vanessa shines the light on her—no monster appendages in sight. She looks like a regular woman wearing old-fashioned clothes. "I was just enjoying sitting in here, listening to sweet Nancy shiver in fear as she lives out the last few moments of her pitiful little life."

"No," Nancy cries, backing into the stone wall where the ladder is attached, leading to the house above. "Stay away from me. Haven't you done enough?"

"Enough?" Clara lets out a genuine laugh, long and

rolling and filled with glee. "You want to cry uncle after seeing a few of your friends get their faces torn off? Nancy, Nancy, Nancy. Who do you think I am?"

Nancy Shaw puts her hands out in front of her—she must have lost her knife somewhere along the way.

"I bet you wish you had this, don't you?" Clara asks, producing the knife from her dress. The blade is identical to the one I'm holding myself. "Don't worry, sister dear." She says the word with disgust. "I wouldn't dream of killing you any other way than how you killed me."

And with that, Clara steps forward and plunges the knife into Nancy's neck. Almost as quickly, she removes it and sinks it in again, this time in the arm, then she moves to the chest, over and over and over again. "How does it feel?" Clara growls, the jovial expression gone, her eyes shining as she continues to stab Nancy. *"How does it feel, you miserable bitch?"*

Nancy makes a few gurgling sounds, fear evident in her widened eyes. "Pleeth," she manages, choking on her own blood. "No m-m-m…"

"No more?" Clara asks, cackling, but this time there is no joy in her laugh. "Oh, Nancy baby, we're only just getting started!"

And with that, Clara lets out a guttural scream as she quickens the pace of the stabs. She goes at Nancy's body again and again, harder each time, the insect-like clickings coming from beneath her skirt once again.

Soon, Clara's screams are anything but human. She pounds away at the bloody mound of flesh and hair wrapped in green and red sequins, until the body starts to break apart.

I look to Vanessa and see that she's hiding her face. "We're going to die," she whimpers, then starts reciting some prayer that I don't recognize; Catholic, maybe.

She doesn't see the shape of Clara's body change as the monster inside comes out, an ever-transforming form of pure terror and insanity; doesn't see Nancy's skull give in to the force of the appendages, collapsing in on itself like a hard candy with a creamy center.

When it's over, the appendages tuck themselves back in and Clara looks human again, except now her face is smeared with fresh blood.

"I'm sorry I lost my temper for a bit there, girls," she says, taking a forceful deep breath and brushing a curl of dark hair off her forehead. "That one was a little personal for me."

"Let us go," Vanessa weeps, still covering her face. I can't look away from the pile that used to be Nancy, steaming in the cold, the bloody sequins glittering away.

"I almost forgot," Clara says, turning back toward the pile. One quilled black appendage slithers out once again, to scoop up Nancy Shaw and shove what's left of her into a small opening between the stones that make up the wall. "*Now* we're even."

"Revenge has been had at last!" comes Penelope's voice from behind us. Vanessa screams and jumps aside, and I step over to her, shining the light back to the third tunnel. My aunt sits crouched in the opening, her expression completely mad. "Now we can start our new lives."

"New lives?" I ask hesitantly, waiting for Clara to move away from the opening of the tunnel that leads out so we can bolt through. I doubt the monster will let us out, but we have to try. "What are you talking about?"

"There's been a change in plans," Clara says, looking down at Penelope with a sort of disgust on her face, like there's a stinking dog sitting on her brand-new carpet. "You can leave, servant."

"But... What?" Penelope asks, devastation painting her previously gleeful face. "No, no, no, you said that if I showed my dedication, if I helped you get revenge..."

"What I *said*," Clara interrupts, her upper lip curling into a snarl, "was that I would make you mine if you were able to do as you were told."

"I have!" Penelope screams, stomping her foot like an upset child. "I've done everything you asked, haven't I?"

"No," Clara says. "You couldn't handle yourself when you saw what else lies in these tunnels, the other lurkers with powers as wondrous as mine. You lost your mind. Look at you now, crouching there in the dark like some sort of rabid animal. You're weak."

"I am not weak!" Penelope wails, collapsing at Clara's feet and grabbing on to her dress with both hands. "I even brought you my own niece, the one you said you couldn't crack yourself. I brought her here just for you!"

My stomach does a flop, threatening to empty its contents. Penelope dragged me down here as a trap.

"And look at her," Clara says, looking at me with… pride? "Everyone I've ever encountered bent to my will and suggestion without a second thought, but not Lucy. She is strong. Stronger than you."

Penelope looks at me with pure hatred, and I try to remember gardening with her when I was young, laughing over tomatoes and cucumbers while Margaret scowled in the background. I have wasted my entire life looking up to Penelope, wishing she was my mother, and looking down on Margaret for disrespecting her. But my cousin was right—Penelope is no mother at all.

"What are you talking about?" I say, and Clara steps away from the mouth of the exit tunnel to look into my face close-up.

"I mean, I choose you," Clara answers, her eyes soft, her tone affectionate. "What is a Mother without a Daughter to teach everything she knows?"

"I'm your daughter!" Penelope rages, crawling toward

me with a strangled cry. I scream and step back, raise the blade at her to no avail, but Clara steps between us.

"You are not." The Mother's warmth ceases as she looks down at my aunt. "You're so pathetic, you'd do anything I said. Anything."

"I've done things for you!" Penelope tries again, standing up before Clara. "I dug up your old students from the cemetery, I pulled their teeth out, I *swallowed* them just to prove my dedication!" She moves forward, like she's going to try to hug the creature in the black dress, but Clara puts her hand up and says firmly, "Stop."

Penelope stops.

"Open your mouth wide," Clara says, and Penelope complies immediately, almost to the point where I wonder if she has any real control at all.

"Now spit them forward," Clara continues, her smile widening wickedly like it did before she attacked the club wives. "Your dedication means nothing to me."

Penelope leans forward and vomits, massively. At first I think it's just regular vomit, but almost immediately I hear the sound of teeth hitting the stone floor, like a bowl of beads that has been overturned. I watch my aunt retch as the teeth come out in thick waves, swimming in green bile, flooding over the stone floor, making scratching noises as they slide aside to make room for more.

When she's finished, my aunt gasps for breath, tears streaming from her eyes, her nose running.

"I think I'd like you to keep going," Clara whispers, and Penelope's eyes widen. "Give me all you've got."

At first, nothing. But then a gurgling sound comes from deep within Penelope's throat. Her eyes widen in disbelief, and then pain, and blood begins to dribble from her lips.

"What's happening?" I cry out, as something thick and pink pushes through Penelope's lips. She leans down, gagging and moaning, until the thing slithers out like a very long snake, piling on the stone floor in swirling coils over the teeth.

Her stomach.

But she's not done. More organs push themselves out of my aunt, spewing forth from her mouth before splattering onto the floor, and I can hardly hear the sound of my own thoughts over Vanessa's screams. I vaguely process that she's taken off through the exit tunnel, without the flashlight, without me. Clara does nothing to stop her.

Good, I think, listening to the sound of her footsteps fade away into the darkness. *At least she got away.*

When my aunt has finished throwing up her guts, she crumples to the floor, dead.

"She wasn't what I needed in a daughter," Clara says, locking eyes with me, holding out her hand in the cold stone room of blood and death. "Her strength was superficial. But something tells me you're differ-ent. Something tells me you'll last forever and ever."

"No," I manage, realizing what it is that Clara is telling me. She lowers her hand back down when I don't take it.

"Yes." The monster is grinning at me. "You'll do it or I'll make those scars you've carved into your body look like butterfly kisses."

"Please..." I fall against the stone wall, my feet so cold I can't feel them anymore. "You can't make me do this."

"But I need new worshippers now, Lucy," Clara says. "All of mine have turned up dead, fancy that. And I know the perfect person to bring the newcomers in, dazzle them with this beautiful estate, tempt them with promises only I can keep..."

I scream out in agony, which only makes her smile widen. All of the things that drove me to hurt myself, all the pressures and expectations that made me miserable— I'm never going to escape them. I'm going to live them forever. *An Acosta must never lack control. She must keep her back straight, and her clothes ironed, and her expression placid. She must refuse to be seen unless her hair and makeup have been set. She wears her armor like scales on a snake: patterned, impervious, perfect. She understands that smiling is tactical, that words are for getting things that you want, that tears have no use except to expose disgusting, snotty shortcomings.*

I will never escape.

"If you run, I will find you," Clara says and steps past me to enter the tunnel that Penelope lured me and Vanessa into minutes ago. "We're linked for eternity now, you and I."

I step away from the woman in the black Victorian dress, weeping, and make my way toward the ladder that will lead back up to the house, to my new life. By the time I reach it, I've grown silent, stoic.

"You're so much stronger than you think," Clara's voice calls after me once I've started climbing, the sound of her appendages clicking excitedly on the stone below. "You'll see what I mean soon enough. You're going to do a wonderful job, Lucy. You're going to make your new Mother very proud."

Only time will tell, I think numbly as I climb rung after rung, the light from the attic barely visible above me. *But time is all I have now.*

Time and this house, which I'll never leave again.

★ ★ ★ ★ ★

ACKNOWLEDGMENTS

THANK YOU, THANK YOU, thank you:

To all of my readers. Your emails and letters and Tweets have a magical way of bringing the biggest smile to my face! I am endlessly grateful for all of you.

To my agent, Joanna Volpe, and to everybody at New Leaf. The amount of hard work you guys do on a daily basis blows my mind to smithereens. I cannot wait to see what other sorts of adventures await us in the future!

To my endlessly supportive editor, T.S. Ferguson. Horror-koalas for life! Also to Siena Konscol, my above-and-beyond publicist, who is made entirely of awesomesauce. And to the entire team at Harlequin TEEN for helping to make my dreams come true. I am such a lucky author to have all of you behind me.

To my wonderful UK team: Rachel Mann of Simon &

Schuster UK, and James Wills of Waston, Little. Thank you for being so enthusiastic and welcoming!

To Gena Showalter and Kate Smith, who provided me with infinite seasoned-author wisdom, happy tears and seriously good times on our adventure across the country together. I love you girls, truly.

To my YA Highway meese—you are all the best.

To Roxie, my sweet and amazing sister-friend.

To Chelsea, who has been by my side since kindergarten. We all float down here, Chels. (In extension, thank you to Alexa and Cassy, who provided me with the best girls' nights ever when writing this book was quite literally driving me insane.) Love you all.

To Edmund, my love and my favorite human. And to Lily and Jude, who make my heart overflow on a daily basis.